Literature

Catfish Karkowsky

Livingston Press
University of West Alabama

Copyright © 2009 Catfish Karkowsky
All rights reserved, including electronic text
isbn 13: 978-1-60489-039-6 library binding
isbn 13: 978-1-60489-040-2 trade paper
Library of Congress Control Number 2009931606
Printed on acid-free paper.
Printed in the United States of America,
Publishers Graphics
Hardcover binding by: Heckman Bindery

Typesetting and page layout: Joe Taylor
Proofreading: Joe Taylor, Jill Harris, Connie James, Joe Taylor
Cover design and layout: Jennifer Brown
Cover Art Bruce New

This is a work of fiction.
Surely you know the rest: any resemblance
to persons living or dead is coincidental.

Livingston Press is part of The University of West Alabama,
and thereby has non-profit status.
Donations are tax-deductible:
brothers and sisters, we need 'em.

first edition
6 5 4 3 3 2 1

Literature

Table of Contents

Real Creamy Ice Cream..1

Women?..4

Stalking's in My Blood...11

Sheriff the Hero..13

The Baby Store..20

Albino God..26

Best Invention Ever...28

I Would Die for Bon Jovi..33

Camp Willpower..37

Father Knows Best...44

Future future 49

The Mother... 51

Kokey Pop 55

Baby License 61

Breakfast Sex 68

Evolve, or the World Evolves Without You 73

Pink Jails 78

The Schizophrenic Mixer..81

Thank You Doctor Shockley..89

Jimmy Dreams...94

Listening to My Son..101
Dara Come Home..105
Soldier Jerry and his Steed Bessie Ann..............109
The Elderly Crisis..116
Grandpa's Grandson...119
Twenty Words For Free Lovin'............................122
Notebook #14..135
Cyrus's Revelation..139
The Robot Garden...143
Mojave 151

Real Creamy Ice Cream

    Remember when that guy came up to you and was like, hey let's have sex, and you were like, I'm not gay, and the guy was like, I'm a girl, and you were like, I don't have sex with strangers from the street, and then the person was like, you know me, I'm your wife we've been married for fifteen years and we have three kids and a house over there near the ice cream store, and you were like, I really like that ice cream store, the ice cream there is real creamy, and she was like, yeah that's why we bought the house, so you could have creamy ice cream every day, and you were like, that was a great idea, I *do* love ice cream.
    And she was like, wasn't that nice of me to let us move there, even though ice cream gives you amnesia.
    And you were like that's *preposterous,* and she was like, I know it must sound that way to you but here's a note from the doctor, and then she took out this note that said you get amnesia from ice cream.
    You looked at it and you were like, hey that's my family doctor from when I was a little kid, and the woman got kind of angry, and was like, *that* he remembers but his own wife he draws a blank. And you were like, I don't know, though, I mean, even if I compromise that ice cream gives me amnesia, I haven't eaten ice cream in a while, maybe months, probably because I'm well aware of my amnesia problem and take pains not to

trigger it, and she was like, what's that in your hand dumbass? But real sarcastic-like because you had an ice cream cone in your hand, and you looked down and you saw that it was an ice cream cone, she hadn't been tricking you at all. You were eating ice cream and it does give you amnesia and she probably is your wife because who else would marry such a brainfuck like you, and then you were like, oh, thank you dear, it *is* an ice cream cone, how silly of me, and then you were about to take a lick of the ice cream because it's one of your favorite flavors–double-chocolate-cherry–but your wife held the ice cream away from your mouth.

As your wife I forbid you to eat more ice cream and lose more memory. Soon your mind will be as blank as vanilla, is what she said.

First you almost punched her, because no one gets in between you and double-chocolate-cherry, not even some two-bit whore who calls herself your wife. She took off her clothes and yelled, I won't be married to a vanilla brain! And you thought that was so funny because here was this woman you didn't even know, taking off her clothes for you in a sacrificial way when, quite honestly, you don't even like yourself. To top it all off: vanilla is your least favorite flavor. It's like white sugar doo-doo, is how you put it.

 While you were laughing she took the ice cream and dumped it down the sewer, and you went diving down there afterwards because of course it's your superduper favorite flavor of ice cream. Then you were down in the sewer for three years because there was no way out. The woman was bringing you sandwiches for a few days and then one day she brought you an ice-cream cone, vanilla, your least favorite, but you ate it anyway because you were so starving and she bent down to the sewer hole and was like, oh sorry wrong guy, and then she left forever, and you were like, hell, story of my life. And I'm just this second guy in your head, not even a real person, just a voice, and let me tell you, there's no doubt that you've gone totally crazy. Remember how I showed you a note from your family doctor that says if you eat vanilla you'll go bonkers. And you were like, hey that's my family doctor from when I was a kid, and I gave you a big hug in your brain because you're so doggone cute sometimes especially when you're double-chocolate-mindless. I'll still be your friend even though you can't remember where you are or what you love, if you love ice cream or cheesecake, and this sewerhole will be your home for all of spotless eternity. Because you're funny, you make me laugh and it reminds me of childhood.

Women?

She kept complaining about how her boyfriend's some asshole, as if I give a shit, so I was like, "Stop yappin already, this dick's not gonna suck itself." Then when she was done I said "Bitch get out" and I kicked her ass out of the car. Then I drove around for a while drinking a 40 then I found half a 40 under the driver's seat, and even though it was flat I drank it and felt pretty good, not drunk but maybe halfway there.

I started thinking a lot in some deep way about all my relationships. Like, how come all the girls I know want me to hit 'em?

So then I was driving round the deader streets downtown kinda swerving around half drunk and I wasn't really paying attention cuz I got this television in my car playing old-school Soul-Train reruns and I cracked this bum out on Maple and he was giving me shit, standing near the car, holding his forehead and there was some blood— "take me to the hospital" and all that bullshit, but I was like, "Hey, you're alright it's no big deal, you're standing and yelling aren't you?"

"No," he says, "my leg isn't working right, you fucked me up." Then he started hobbling around all jerky and then he kicked my bumper. I laughed because you could tell his leg was alright, old man was putting on a show, but then all of a sudden I got really pissed that he was lying and wasting my time and I just put

$800 into my piece of shit car a month ago to fix its transmission when it was blowing this purple smoke into the car that made me dizzy but not good dizzy, puke dizzy.

When the bum sat on the hood, I got out of the car and was like, "You better stop that old man or I'll knock your head off." Then he started that old grandma trick, "Boo hoo I'll call the police," so I socked him one right in the teeth, laid him out flat on the hood. Then I got in the car and started it up and he was staggering around in front, not letting me drive. He was bleeding and spitting out all this blood, trying to get his rancid homeless bloody saliva on my car. He even spit some on my windshield, so Ba-bam! I ran the old fucker over into the pavement. Then he was lying on the middle yellow line and I was looking him over, he wasn't too big I guess, and I heard this front door slam a few houses away, and I didn't wanna deal with any good citizen shit, so I picked him up and threw his body in the trunk.

I was surprised because, man, he stank like shit! I just wanted to dump his old ass in the forest or something, but then on the way to Shelby he woke up and started raising a racket, got hold of the tire iron and was banging it like a madman against the bottom of the trunk, so I decided to take him home. They got these guard booths here and there on those smaller roads and I get pulled over every other day. When a cop sees my car he thinks, There's some guy with a dick twice as big as mine. Then it's all over. Every cop sees I got *big dick* written all over me.

My night was shit anyway because I stank from touching the guy's raincoat and I figured if I smoked the old guy up and poured him a cold beer he might settle down and there wouldn't be any trouble in the morning. Then, like an hour later, the old guy was hangin' out on the couch and smoking pot and laughing at the MTV whenever the girls were dancing in their bikinis and then my old lady smelled the pot from down the hall, and she was like, "When are you gonna get serious, you good-for-nothing! I was working twelve hours a day in the mattress factory at your age." But she knows I make good money selling that weed. How else could I buy that Escalade I cracked up? I can't keep riding that bike around the neighborhood or I fall when I drink. If I need to sleep I can pull the car over, but with a bike I wake up on some guy's lawn with a shotgun at my face. Plus I keep plenty of cigarettes around the house and pizza and hamburgers in the oven which she's always shoving into her toothless face and how come she thinks that shit grows on trees? So then she shuffled into the room in her slippers and blue night gown that she never changes out of and she saw the old guy, and was like, "Why is there a godawful streetbum in my house smoking marijuana, has the world gone insane? And his head all cut up too..."

Then she felt all bad and she heated up all these towels and took out all these Flintstones vitamins and other medicine and shit, pretending she's some kind of modern day Betsy Ross nurse, like she's gonna heal him like a saint, even though this lady, I swear, picks her scabs and eats them, I've seen it. So then this old homeless guy, he sees he's got someone listening to him finally for the first time in years and he starts complaining how bad his head is hurting and how his balls ain't been rubbed for twenty years and how he needs to go the hospital for all kinds of shit but he can't because he smoked crack before I ran him over and the hospital tests'll show it and the doctors'll take him to jail. So I went off on him, even brought out my gun, because this guy's smoking borrowed pot and I can see my mom making plans for a third marriage, so I was like, "Man, *I* didn't tell you to do hard drugs this morning, everyone knows you stick to weed. That's probably why you walked in the middle of the goddamn street right in front of my car."

Then my mom took the bum's side. She's seen my gun too many times to be afraid and she'll take any excuse to get on my case. "You need to treat your elders better, especially when you're the host who brought him by. I didn't raise my son to be a good-for-nothing drug dealer who can't even act like a decent host." Then she turned to the guy, and was like, "I'm sorry mister for my son's poor manners. He sure didn't pick those up from me. He hung out in a bad crowd in high school and now he's all kinds of trouble. I'm fed up with it and it's out of my hands."

See, I had enough of that BS because my mom's always on my case even though she can't even take care of herself, so I was like, "Go back to watching your Home Shopping Channel and buying your fucking china dolls and glass animals. That's *my* damn money." Then she went berserk for twenty minutes throwing all those glass animals, or ceramic, or whatever it is she buys. Kittens with balls of yarn, puppies rolling in the grass, baby cows with giant eyes trying to stand on skinny legs, she was throwing them all around until the floor was covered with broken animal pieces. That was about $1200 worth of glass animal crap. And she even cracked the bum on the head with some cute-as-hell Bambi and she fell on her knees in front of him and started crying, kissing him and everything. But I couldn't take it cuz the dude smelled like a cesspool, so I said, "Nu-uh I don't want this smelly old bum in the house anymore," so I took him back to the car and was about to toss him in the trunk and he's like, "Don't sweat it, chief, let me sit up front and I'll act OK," but I wasn't about to have that old guy's smelly ass on my refurbished naugehyde, so I hosed him down and we waited around till he dried off and I found him some clothes off the neighbor's clothesline.

In the car, it turned out the guy was alright, pretty smart even and I was glad that I brought along a joint so we could have a deep discussion. He was like, "I wish you hadn't interrupted that TV watching. That was an interesting program on ESPN 3. I'm mostly attracted to gymnasts where you can't tell the breasts from the shoulders."

I guess that was funny but I wasn't in the mood to laugh. "You know," I said, "I believe in God because of women's beach volleyball," which isn't a joke at all but God's honest truth.

Then he asked me, "Have you ever seen a really hot girl in a boxing match? *That's* grace under fire."

"No I never did," I said, "but my dad was some kind of trainer before he ran off."

So then this bum tells me how he plans on marrying my mother, and then he gets all hopeful and goes, "How would you feel if I was your daddy?" and I was like, "How would I feel? I'd feel like I had a daddy that stank like shit. I'd feel like there'd be another sack of piss who eats my hamburgers." I was getting pretty heated at that point and I made it clear that I already had one dad and he wasn't worth shit, why replay the obvious?

So this bum says, "I could help you with school and keep books for your drug deals. I got a college degree in accounting."

And I was like, "Who the fuck's in school?" cuz I haven't been in school in five years unless I'm dropping off some dope to some fucked up kids. I said to the bum, "I left school cuz they were only teaching me how *not* to make money. And I fucking hate reading. All those little words. All those tiny words."

So then he says, "You don't know the world, you need a daddy to make you go to school. You're Mom wants what's good for you and you can't see it. If you were a daddy you would know."

"Hell yeah, I probably am," I said. I've never used a condom in my life, and I've slept with twenty-six girls, all of them fucked up, and all of them trying to have babies to share that fuckedupness. I've seen my ex-girlfriends with some googly-eyed babies almost as handsome as me, but they'll never pin me unless they get me DNA-tested on Maury Povich. In school they gave us a whole talk about safe sex but I'm not gonna run out to spend five bucks in the heat of the moment. That's not worth the trouble cuz the girl's asleep by the time you get back or maybe foolin around with one of your friends. And the free condoms from the clinic are thick as hell. Fucking with them is like kicking a girl in the groin with a pair of galoshes.

So then I was hoping this old guy gave up on being my dad which was the right thing to do, but he starts fiddling with my radio stations like he owns my car, and to be honest, I don't like people touching anything in my car, not even the seatbelts or the door handles. I even like them sitting on newspapers. So I stopped the car right there, we were somewhere in the middle of the forest, and I was like, "OK, old man, time to hit the road."

So the guy doesn't wanna get out, he's telling me a hard luck story about his first wife running off and how he lost his job twenty years ago, but I wasn't impressed. Twenty years is a long time to be feeling out the job market if you ask me. So I decide I'm gonna haul his ass out of the car, and when he sees me getting out, he climbs out on his own and looks around at all these trees and bushes and birds and squirrels or whatever. There's nothing out there, man, like totally nothing, and he's like, "If you leave me here in the middle of nowhere I'm still going back to your momma's house tomorrow. I memorized the address and I'm gonna marry your momma and I'll be your daddy whether you like it or not cuz your mother is an honest and generous woman who needs and deserves companionship and nothing can stop true love."

And I told the guy he better not come by or I'll cut his balls off and switch them for his eyeballs, but then a week later I'm coming home after a full day, a bad day, dealing with this guy who keeps thinking that I give weed away for free instead of trying to make a profit, and I see this bum's going in my front door dressed in a thrift-store corduroy suit, trying to look like a macked out Bill Clinton, and he's got a bunch of flowers he grabbed from the neighbor's lawn.

I stay in the car thinking how I'm gonna scare the living shit out of this guy so I'll never see him again, and then I go over to the window quietly and inside I see my mom getting all giggly and she runs upstairs to get dressed for some date. I had to wait a while in the bushes, like maybe an hour, and all the while the guy's sitting on the couch watching MTV and fiddling with himself and then he took a hamburger from the oven, and I almost rushed in there to crack his head like a piñata. Then my mom comes down wearing all this white makeup like a clown and a sequin dress on top of her blue nightgown, and she's got these fake pearl earrings and some weird dance slippers.

So they both set out to Rocketburger in a taxi and I follow them and they're having a good time, eating, laughing, kissing and everything and my mom looks pretty happy and then when my mom went to use the bathroom, I crept in there and told the guy to take a hike and never come back. I waved my gun in his face and my friend Victor had his baton and Victor's about the baddest looking dude in town cuz his face is all scarred up from some fire, and then he just takes these steroids all day and lifts weights so he has a neck like a dump truck. Victor screamed cuz I got him all worked up and he even punched himself in the head, and the bum knew right away I wasn't kidding.

Then when I got home I heard my mom crying. I thought about maybe apologizing and finding the guy to come back, or some other guy who didn't smell as bad, just so my mom's life is not as shitty, but I think it's better. She's a soft woman and easy to take advantage of. Plus you can't let all kinds of people into your private life, even pretty smart bums who deserve a break. People turn on you, and that's a fact. It's not cuz their bad but just because they're people. That's what we do. Fucking people over is in our bones.

Stalking's in My Blood

My grandpapa was a stalker, my grandpapa's grandpapa was a stalker and I'm a stalker. I stalk because it's in my blood and it's what I love to do. I'd rather be stalking than anything. Sometimes when I'm up in a tree, or on top of a roof keeping tabs on a special girl, I'll just look up into the sky and think: God, today I feel like the luckiest bastard alive. Lou Gehrig's got nothing on me.

For my first birthday my parents bought me a size-zero black ski mask. When I was three they bought me a zipwire. When I turned five they bought me Native-American silent-step moccasins. At seven, they got me my first pair of Kevlo double-focus black-diamond binoculars. At twelve they bought me a utility belt. When I turned fifteen they got me a set of surveillance cameras. All in all, I've had a lot of stalking encouragement.

Now I don't want to give you the wrong impression. I'm no Grandmaster Stalker that gets talked about for years. Foppman from Darnsville who stalked Mary Cahane and her daughter and granddaughter over six decades, or Sneaky Snelling who stalked Leah Pralines with such persistence that when he suddenly stopped, she began stalking him, wondering why.

But, still, I'm a pretty good stalker. I've been told my moves have certain panache, ripe for legacy. My parents even stalked each other for a time. My dad waited for my mom behind the front yard bushes while my mom waited for my dad behind the backward hedges. And I hope one day my son will grow to appreciate the family art. And even if I have a daughter, also her.

Right now I'm stalking a girl named Frannie and I hope to make some progress in a relationship by the year's end when I'll finally introduce myself. I am currently amassing my third journal on Frannie of extraordinarily personal demographic information. I know her shoe size, waist size, food preferences. I know how often she has sex and that she cries afterwards each time. I've made contact with her extended family in Buenos Aires and I know that her Portuguese is very limited.

But I always try to keep in mind that I'm different than Foppman and all the others. The day I catch Frannie is the day I retire from the stalking business. What's the use of making myself lawless for the rest of life? Some of these other guys jump from one stalking gig to the next, in an addicted way, never settled down, never satisfied. You have to love the thing when you catch it, is what I believe, *really* love it, for what it is, or all the pursuit was just a lie. People get too obsessed with obsession. But not me. I'll promise Frannie that she's the one, the ultimate stalker's dream and that devotion to her was all I was ever after.

Little pieces here and there, that's the key. It's in my blood, after all, and forgetting stalking would be like living a lie. When I have my family, I'll stalk Frannie in a way she won't know, my kids, too, so it won't infringe on their lives. I'll stalk my boss ever so slightly so that he won't even know it's there. I'll look just like a regular guy to everyone. No one will know my true love, my true devotion to stalking, even though, bit by bit, I'll practice it everyday, quietly in love.

Sheriff the Hero

The man called Stoner Twiggy—'as thin as a starving mountain cat,' he would say about himself with a gap-toothed grin—sat on a log at the Sun Brothers Commune fire pit. He watched little Johnny absentmindedly poke the burned-out ashes with a stick. Johnny None was shirtless and shoeless and with a grimy face.

"Hey, kid, whatsup?" Twiggy had stiff yellow hair, a bony nose, and a rounded poorly-shaven chin. He was a man of scope and profundity, a man who wanted nothing more than Peace and Weed for the world and the Good of Mankind. He waved towards Johnny, "Come sit around Uncle Twiggy. I wanna tell you a story."

Johnny None jumped up, smacked Twiggy with his stick and then ran in a circle around the ring of rocks that designated the fire pit area. Twiggy's eyes twinkled watching the boy's frenetic energy. He adjusted his denim vest and tucked his sandals beneath him so that he sat cross-legged in the dust.

"So, listen, Johnny, man. *Sit down*, dude." Twiggy said, "You're like running around like a maniac on PCP. Man, a little kid like you shouldn't be doing PCP." Twiggy cracked a wry smile, "I'm kidding, dude. Where you get those tie-dye shorts, man? That's fashionable. Come and sit down here, man. I wanna tell you about the day the commune almost died.

"I mean, this is, like, our whole history, dude, and you don't even know how close it came to ending. Like *so* close. The guy who saved the day was this little boy named Sheriff. I mean, now he's a grown man, Sheriff. Y'know. He's that tall guy with the sideburns and leather vest that walks around with the guitar and the pretty girl named Lilac."

Twiggy paused and soberly picked his teeth with a fingernail, "Man, I loved that girl." He pointed his pinkie at Johnny, "But you know I stepped aside for Sheriff, man, because Sheriff is *the man*. He saved our commune. You don't even know, Johnny-boy. You wouldn't even *be* here. I mean, I wouldn't be here either, man. I'd be sucking gas fumes at a filling station somewhere in Oklahoma. Can I tell you what's in Oklahoma besides filling stations, gas fumes, and a fat ex-girlfriend named Joanne? NA-DA. Nothing. Don't go there, man. It's the pits."

Twiggy paused dramatically and looked towards Johnny, "So, like, that's why you gotta dig what Sheriff did. It's our history. It's, like, the whole world.

"Man. So here it is, I'm gonna lay it out. It started with the Big Fight. Like *this* big, man." Twiggy positioned his hands a meter apart, "It was so fucked up."

Johnny shuffled into a cross-legged position. Twiggy's eyes sparkled and he continued, "See, Amos Desert-Lizard, this dude that died two years ago from trichinosis, he had like this sister or this aunt, Trilly, way back when. And Trilly was a far out chick, man. Not far out, like, awesome, but, like, far out, like 'Where are you, Trilly? Where is your brain?' And she'd be like, 'I'm counting hairs on the cactus spirit.' And you'd be like '*Whoa—* you are a far out lady.'" Twiggy shook his head.

"Whoa. Anyway, she's gone now but she grew this sparkly, leafy grass that was amazing. I mean, like, *wicked amazing*. It was called Puffer Paradise. Just thinking about it makes me feel, like great, inside, like *this*, like so great and loose." He juggled his appendages until they were slack and bouncing. Johnny None giggled. "I could bathe in that stuff, dude, and feel happier than a pig in Truffle-land. Nutty said it came from the Amazon Rainforest, like the bottom part that has all these rich nutrients in the soil, and it got brought up here by some Mexican caballero with a six-shooter and then it was blessed by a Mojave Medicine man. And you know Nutty never lies. *Never*. Man, he *can't*, or he goes impotent for a month.

"So, listen. CloudPuff, the scrawny chick with the buckteeth." Twiggy tilted his head and looked for a sign of recognition in Johnny's face, "You know, the chick with the headcovering." Johnny nodded and Twiggy continued, "Y'know because she's always chattering, if you ask me, too much about her personal feminine hygiene and lunar cycles, cuz, you know, that's not any of my business.

"Well, anyways, she thought Trilly wasn't sharing her Puffer Paradise with her on purpose. Like, she was just doling it out pharmacy-style to everybody, including yours truly, but you know, not to CloudPuff. And CloudPuff was like, 'Hey, how come I'm not partaking of this magic maryjane that everyone's raving about.' You know, cuz we were raving. I mean, oh shit, man, that stuff was good. Man, if only you tried some."

The memory washed over Twiggy and his eyes rolled back in reverie, "Oh Lord, I think I need to do some Zen before I go on."

Johnny None thought the story was over. He stood and began to walk away. Twiggy's eyes popped open, "Wait, Johnny, don't move, I'm here and now man. I was just kidding." Johnny sat down and Twiggy continued.

"So, like, the reason CloudPuff thought that Trilly was holding back was because this little dude, Bunyan, was sleeping with Trilly and then CloudPuff stole him away. He was like a little dude, like he wore a cowboy hat and chaps, these leather chaps, like a Western motif thing, which was stupid if you ask me but he got a lot of chicks. Go figure. Anyway, CloudPuff made him all this stuff. Moccasins and some baskets and like a tree-flute, or something, so Bunyan was all about CloudPuff. And Trilly was, like, angry with CloudPuff. Like, *angry*. Cuz, like, she thought CloudPuff was into stealing men. I don't know if you know Trilly. She's got a big old ugly head like an acorn squash and, man, it was like, bright red, like an acorn squash tomato. I mean, I thought they were gonna fight, man. People were so tense.

"But CloudPuff was like, 'Hey, you know, I don't believe in labels and stuff. I mean, if he's married or something, that's not up to me, cuz I won't even call him my boyfriend. I don't believe in that.' But then, later, they were talking about having this love-child. CloudPuff couldn't decide if she wanted, like, a coffee child, or a chocolate child. She feels really strong about spreading color, man. Like through her womb and stuff. But, like, which color, cuz there's a million and two.

"But then this Puffer Paradise bloomed in Trilly's garden, it just opened up its magic candy womb, with all its beautiful candy, man, and so Bunyan went back to Trilly. In the end, CloudPuff ended up having a pink child, like, I mean, she had a kid with me, and I'm sorta pink and tan, which is like as good a color as any, and so we had this love-child. And, I mean, I definitely love her, but I don't know if I'm *in* love with her. And the kid is like, you, or something, or the other kid, Jimmy. I'm like your dad, or your half dad, if we believed in that stuff on the commune." Twiggy patted Johnny on the head.

"But, anyway, kid, back to the story. Bunyan went back to Trilly because, I mean, cuz he loved her but also because this grass was, like, the grass of all grasses. Like, the uber-grass that the Olympian Gods smoked. And he even kept the moccasins, man. The CloudPuff moccasins.

"So, CloudPuff, like, I mean, she like, burned up all of Bunyan's stuff. I guess she wasn't OK with sharing men like she thought. Bunyan got into her blood or something. She had this big pile of his shit and she was throwing it all into the communal fire and singing and dancing like a scary Native American Sorceress. Some Wicca shit or something. Man, I don't know. I stayed in my tent for like two days after that. I felt tense from that witch-stuff. I mean, I dig good witches. I'm down with all people. But, like, the bad witches, man. I mean, that's just bad for the Mojo. I got kinda impotent. I mean, just for a month. So, that's why I think maybe Jimmy is my kid and not you. I mean, not that it matters.

"Anyway, Bunyan saw the fire of his stuff and he ran, man. He just ran. Just high-tailed it the hell out of here wearing nothing but a nightshirt. No one knew where he went or what happened to him. It was just the desert, the cactus spirits, Bunyan and his nightshirt. And I mean, I got out of my tent and was like 'Bunyan, run, man, RUN!' but then CloudPuff was giving me these dirty looks so I just went back in my tent and kept quiet. But, hell man, the truth is that I can't say I even blame him."

Twiggy scratched his nose and frowned as he remembered the incident.

"Then later, we are all puffing up compliments of Trilly, and CloudPuff walks by, and she's like 'Hey, whatsup? No one, like, informed me of this puff session.' I kept my mouth shut, but Billy Budd was like, 'Man, you're a mood killer, all that *witch* stuff,' and CloudPuff, her face got all wrinkly, like a raisin, and she started crying, and Marjory was like, 'Billy, you're an asshole. Bunyan was a big fat whore.' And GingerRoot was like, 'No one told CloudPuff to start with Bunyan. That was, like, her choice.' And Charley, the girl, Charley, with the purple eyes and purple hair, well, she was like, 'She didn't know he was like that. Bunyan just turned out like that.' 'No way,' said Billy Budd. He took a long drag from the joint and goes, 'Man, *I* knew he was an asshole. Everyone knew it. He was always stealing everyone's waterjugs. Isn't that right, Twiggy?' And, man, I was not digging the tenseness man, what with that delicious ganja to smoke on, so I go, 'Man, no comprende the ingles.' Which is, like, my joke. Y'know, my thing.

"But no one was laughing. Everyone was, like, split up, and I thought the commune was dead, man, *dead*. All the chicks went to one side, and all the dudes to the other, and Twiggy was stuck in the middle. Man, I was so sad. Everybody was yelling and saying shit about men being pigs and women being pigs. And I was like, 'Dude, I will never get laid again,' Y'know. I wasn't impotent then, and not now either, but in the middle I was, I think, but just all this talk about pigs and hate was not good for love.

"And everyone was, like, totally high strung and tense. Man, stress is where it was *at*. And the chicks were like hiding Wicca-pills in our food to make us impotent and like, dizzy at night, and like, the worst diarrhea you ever had, like, we were at the poop-holes all day long, and like, that dude, Billy Budd, he, like, snuck into Marjory's tepee at night and whizzed on her collection of feathers. But I think that was because on Christmas she told everyone he had a small dick.

"But, Johnny, listen man," Twiggy implored with two open hands, "I thought we were goners. All that name-calling, and Bad-Wicca, and diarrhea, and whizzing on the feathers. And at night I could hear Lilac crying, man, and it damn near broke my heart in two. And, I was packing, man. My duffle and my moose-horns. I was getting ready to go.

"But, Dude, get this. This kid Sheriff came out of the back this one day. And he was just a young kid, like eight years old, just like you Johnny, and he was like 'Man, nobody fight. Like, this is about peace, man. Bunyan was the devil, and he started this, but he's, like, gone. And we should just get down with peace.'"

Twiggy clapped his hands and jumped up, "And that's that, man. I mean, I'm hungry so I cut the story short a little. But that's basically it. A kid named Sheriff saved the day. And now he's with Lilac. And, I mean, that Lilac is a pretty woman. But I don't grudge that man Sheriff, cuz he's my hero."

Johnny None stood up. Twiggy took him by the shoulders and gazed into the distance.

"We'll eat in a second, dude, but just listen to this last piece man. It's like, I told that story, because, man, it's got a moral, dude. I mean, there's wisdom here, I mean, we learn *so* much from that historical story because Sheriff is like, in you. I mean, he's part of your spirit. Because he's, like, a hero.

"And he's, like, in me, also. And he's also my hero. And, I mean, sometimes I think I'm my own hero. And, like, you're my hero too, and I'm, like, inside you and you're, like, inside me. I mean, we're each other's heroes, man, and we're also our own heroes and we're even Sheriff's heroes. So, like, let's go eat cuz we all gotta keep on trucking."

With that, Twiggy squeezed Johnny's shoulder and gave him a satisfied nod. He turned and walked towards the dusty circle of the food area where Purple Charley and GingerRoot prepared lunch. Johnny None stood and followed behind, dragging his stick in the dirt.

The Baby Store

"If I were you I wouldn't take either of them. Gutterbabies are dirty; they drink sewage water and eat sewage waste."

"Well, we'd *prefer* a forestbaby, you understand. But we're getting desperate. Couldn't we take a gutterbaby home and clean it up? Would it be normal then? I've heard the dirt's only surface-deep and then we'll teach him how to live on normal clean water."

"Nope, nope." The clerk vigorously shook his head. He was a cleanshaven older man wearing a plain blue T-shirt and a baseball cap. Black stains crossed the T-shirt horizontally at his large paunch. "That's bad information you got."

"OK, well, we're mostly interested in a forestbaby. We figured that at least a forestbaby would know how to scavenge a bit for food, so it would be healthier on the whole."

The clerk shuffled through a stack of order forms on the Baby Store glass counter.

"Maybe so, we've found that forestbabies can be left alone for three weeks and still manage for themselves with natural foraging skills. But they're not domesticated. They'll bite."

The clerk presented a stack of invoices. He shuffled through them and took out two, one for a forestbaby and one for a gutterbaby. The forestbaby invoice had a photo clipped to its corner: a beautiful soft-skinned baby with wide wild eyes.

"You have to understand that you can't ever clean up a gutterbaby. They always have the gutter in them. Sometimes a couple'll bring 'em in here to have 'em cleaned up and deodorized and these people don't understand: the gutterbaby comes like that, that stink is *in* them."

The customer gave a concentrated look to show that he listened carefully. His wife, a short woman in a bright yellow jumper and pageboy haircut, roved the store displays. 'Oh!' she exclaimed and then sighed.

Her husband turned to watch as she scanned an advertisement for an officebaby. Her lips murmured as she read. He shook his head and hoped she would notice. She acted like a drugged woman these past months; talked about nothing but babies. She had filled the storage closet with rattles, bottles, tubs of powder, tiny blue and pink pajamas with footsies, bright hanging carousels. He felt angry and impotent that she was mooning over the expensive babies that they could never dream of affording.

She leaned into the display-crib arranged along the wall of the store, wrinkled up her nose, and cooed lovingly at the rosycheeked storebaby. 'Goo-*goo*-gah-*gah*,' she said in an affected baby-voice imitation.

The man looked apologetically at the clerk. He was prematurely balding and wore a short-sleeved polo-shirt and golfing khakis. "My wife was willing to settle for a gutterbaby. She went baby crazy about two months ago and I was hoping it would pass. Then, at least, I convinced her to do some research. I figured you don't want to jump into these things."

The clerk grunted.

The store bell suddenly jingled and a well-dressed couple entered, conversing brightly. The store clerk watched them drift to a display before he impatiently turned to the man.

"I thought if we waited a few days a forestbaby might pop up. Maybe we'd even be lucky and run across one in the Wheaton forest." He smiled, "We've been walking three hours everyday, almost eight miles. It seems the forests are empty these days."

The clerk raised his hand and furrowed his brow in the way an expert prepares a speech, "I have to tell you, sir—"

The man interrupted, "It's not like forestbabies are ideal either, but it's really our only chance."

"...You won't find one around here. They're all harvested years ago. That's number one. We collected a good crop of forestbabies from the Burma delta last month. They're in nursery-storage in Nebraska as we speak. If you wanna come back in a week and check, I can put you down on my list today..."

The customer's wife joined them at the counter. She leaned towards the clerk and listened to the men's conversation. Her face shone with interest and emotion.

"...they're small, fairly clean, straight from the bush. If you've decided on a forestbaby it's a pretty good value."

"You should see," she pulled on her husband's sleeve, "they have these moonbabies now. It's crazy, they're green, and they *glow*. At night they glow."

"Yes ma'am, that's the new model this year. It's expected to be pretty popular. They have a beautiful green-yellow glow, but we find, on the other hand, they get sick sometimes with earth food."

The woman pursed her lips in apology, "We could never afford it. I just thought it was really cool."

"Honey," the husband grasped her wrist and elbow, as if to silence her, and drew her close, "this man was about to give us some prices on forestbabies."

The woman instantly quieted.

He took a laminated spreadsheet of numbers from behind the desk and studied it with his pointer finger. "Well, we can offer you a farmbaby for twenty-thousand dollars."

The woman gasped and shook her head. "Oh, no, that's way

way too much."

"What about those forestbabies?" the man implored, ". . .the ones from Bermuda…"

"Hmm… Those are from Burma and they're selling pretty well. There's a pretty long waiting list here. I don't know if it's even worth adding your name…"

The man raised his chin, "But how much are they?" His wife's knuckles whitened on the counter edge. She strained against her husband's grasp. It felt as though she would jump across the counter to assault the clerk.

"Those are twelve thousand each."

"Oh, no." The woman let out a sigh. "That's way too much, way *way* too much." Her face darkened, like a defeated child.

"Honey," the husband took his wife's shoulder.

"What?" Her voice cracked. He discreetly turned her towards the exit and whispered gently as he guided her outside.

The well-dressed couple approached the counter. They both wore black. Only the woman wore color, a dark crimson scarf, setting off her black sweater from her raven hair. The man's salt and pepper hair was gelled into a handsome wave. The clerk guessed that he was a decade older than the woman.

The man spoke first, "We've been looking around and we're interested in a baby."

The woman continued, "But we don't have much to spend."

"Did you have a particular one in mind?"

"Not an individual baby. But we liked the carbabies you have back there." The woman turned and pointed, "They seem nice enough."

"Well, we offer all kinds, so you'd want to choose carefully. A courtroombaby is relatively inexpensive and can be a very good investment. We'll be getting a shipment within the next few months. But I gotta tell you that I've promised most of them away already. If you're comfortable making a down payment of $500 today, I'll see what I can do."

"When will you know?"

"Definitely by October."

The woman whispered into the man's ear, took his hand to her mouth, and gently kissed his knuckle. "Let's not wait, honey, let's get one now."

"I've got a handful of storebabies, that one there is on sale…" He pointed to the crib-display. Neither of them turned to look. "…and one or two carbabies for $20,000 each..."

"That's out of our budget."

The clerk was surprised. The man had looked, at first glance, like a big spender. The couple continued staring without flinching. The bell chimed and the polo-shirted man re-entered without his wife. He loitered by the display advertisements, waiting for the clerk. Wet marks, which could only be his wife's tears, stained his shirt at the shoulder. The clerk considered rushing this older couple. Something told him that a sale would go down with this other man.

"You don't want to spend too low, or you'll get a lemon." He pursed his lips and let this suggestion sink in, "Most customers are happy with their churchbabies."

"Oh, I'd love a singer!" The woman smiled broadly.

"No, I don't need any of that holier-than-thou stuff when he's a teenager."

The clerk saw that the man's interest had waned. "Why don't you take another look around the store and I'll be with you in a few minutes."

The couple nodded and left to look at the displays. The polo-shirted man approached the counter. Behind him, the well-dressed couple immediately left, chiming the bell.

"What do you have?"

"All I can offer you is a junkbaby for two thousand or a

dumpbaby for one thousand. Gutterbabies are going for five hundred but I'm doing you a favor by not selling you one. Believe me."

The man glanced behind him. His wife paced the sidewalk in front of the store entrance. Impulsively, he decided, "Listen, write me down for a junkbaby. We'll take one of those."

"Okey-doke. You need to fill this out." He slid a clipboard towards the man with a triple-layered carbon form on top. The man took the pen and hunched over the form.

"And there's a two hundred dollar deposit."

The man nodded without looking up. Slowly, as if in pain, he brought out his wallet and placed two crisp one-hundred dollar bills on the counter. He handed the form over. The clerk guessed that the bills had only that morning been withdrawn from the bank. When the man left, the clerk watched through the store window as he told his wife. She threw her arms around him and kissed him on the neck. The clerk filed the order and put the hundred dollar bills in the cash register. Before locking the Baby Store for the night, he fed the storebaby and washed the makeup from its face.

Albino God

Black people should only look at black pornography! White people should only get off on white snuff films! Good people, don't confuse your lust, keep to your own masturbations!

I'm sorry that I'm a racist. I don't have any black friends because I grew up in China and I don't have any Chinese friends because I'm an albino. Albinos are clearly the most superior race on Earth. I'm not saying that *your* race isn't superior, I certainly don't wish to fight, but clearly the superiority of your race is an inferior sort of superiority when compared to the albino. With that almost transparent skin, endowed randomly like a genie's wish on individuals equally from all people, what can't an albino do? Nothing, that's what…Albinos should be given the reins to the world. Albinos are the strongest, the fastest, the smartest, the most good-looking.

Albino brothers! Hear my call! We should only hang out with true races! Midgets and hermaphrodites! And maybe the race of retarded people too!

Sometimes when I see a dark white person or a light black person I think: Impure admixture of blood! Contaminated genetics!

Not so with albinos. We are as pure as the unplowed snow, as untarnished as the cloudless morning sky. Once born, we cannot be tainted.

What is the most unfortunate fact about an albino's life? It is that two albinos mating will not necessarily have an albino child... How sad that such a beautiful act, the greeting of melatonin-less genitals should not produce an equally beautiful offspring... Sometimes when I see a beautiful albino couple with a normal child I feel terrible for the state of this world which continuously robs our already deficient planet of still more beauty.

But I have created a machine for which I deserve the Nobel Prize. It is a eugenetic-machine which sorts out and eradicates all non-albino DNA. Whether you're white, black, Latino, Asian, purple or green, with my machine any two parents can be assured they will not have to proliferate the ugliness of their own pigment-stains or some mixture in between. Then they will surely gain the favor of the almighty Albino God.

Best Invention Ever

The best invention ever is the blowjob. The second best invention is paper. The third best invention is the fax machine. The fourth is antibiotics. Number ten is Hamburger Helper. Number fifty is Sixty-Nine. The last best invention is the Internet. Internet would have been higher on the list but for an invention to really be great it's gotta be elitist. Girls can't get blowjobs which is why blowjobs scored so high. People always want stuff they can't have. The Jealousy-Factor is integral for the best invention list. Everybody can have Internet so who wants it?

That's also why antibiotics scored lower. Because everybody can take it unless they don't have any orifices like my friend Seal. They call him Seal because he's 'sealed up.' He's sort of pod-shaped and appendage-less. You could mistake him for a really big potato except for the fact that he wiggles around a lot. They have to feed him through an artificial hole in his belly, of course it's not really his belly, it's just the flatter part of the pod-shape. They also take out the waste from the artificial hole. The food and the waste are the same thing. In a way Seal just likes to cozy up with food for a short time. Since he can't communicate with words or hand-signals, he just lets people know what he wants from the artificial hole. When he's hungry he gives off a hungry smell, when he wants to be around trees he gives off that smell, when he needs to be rolled into the sun, etc…

They used to call him Pod but he gave off a sour smell, like rotten eggs, and it was understood that he didn't like that name. For awhile, Seal had a robot body (Best Invention #24) where he could sit in a basket and move around like a normal person. The robot had these arms and legs that Seal could maneuver when they hooked up neuron circuits to his brain (not really the brain but the rounder part of the pod-shape). That robot frame was pretty kickass. Seal even took over the world for a little while, maybe like ten minutes. If you missed it, it's because it was in the middle of the night Pacific Standard Time. Most people were sleeping so they didn't know that Seal was holding the world hostage, but then he got hungry and he remembered that the robot arms only had these pincers that were no good for preparing snacks. He had to wake up his mom. The pincers could pick up stuff OK and if you had a can it could pop that sucker's lid off in a second, but it could never get a handle on simple things like mixing stuff or holding a cup. So that's why his tenure as world dictator was so short.

Afterwards, his mom took the robot body away from him because he was so dangerous and he went back to wiggling around in the sun and generally getting in the way. His mom kinda preferred him in that form, if you ask me, because she always had someone to yell at. But she wasn't wrong; he always seemed to be under your foot no matter where you were walking, bathroom, attic, closet, everywhere. I know you feel bad for the guy and you probably think I'm some sort of asshole, but you shouldn't. Nature, nurture, bullshit, Seal was a bad person through and through. Man, *I* wouldn't try to take over the world if I had a robot body. Maybe I'd wreak havoc on a CATscan machine or an arch-nemesis or maybe ride around on a missile, but nothing like trying to bring slavery to the human race! Shit!

Anyway, Seal's one of the few people I know who wishes he could take antibiotics. He's got a smell which just reeks of

'Hell, I wish I could take antibiotics.' Y'know because he's jealous. Here's a slogan for an antibiotics company, *Antibiotics: great invention… almost as good as the blowjob.* What do you think?

In my backyard I've made a shrine to the woman who first invented blowjobs. She was really a Neanderthal so I don't know if she's technically a woman, more like a monkey-woman, which explains why she was so horny. Her name was Pernok and she was the mother of Eve. I think she may have had sex with God. It's in the Bible somewhere, like towards the beginning or maybe it's from the prequel, in the backstory where God sets up the plot. I think it talks about when God was sitting around with nothing to do and you can just feel the tension rising. When I was reading through that I said to myself, 'Man, *that* dude's gonna create something *any* second now.' You could just tell. Because, anyway, what can you do when there's nothing around except maybe twiddle your thumbs and masturbate godstyle. Hell, there weren't even soliloquies created yet (BI #65). Another theory is that God created the world while he was on the toilet. That's where all my best ideas come from.

Anyway, if the name Pernok sounds familiar it's because she's also the one who invented porn (BI #9). There's these charcoal drawings on a cave wall in France that are 20,000 years old. They've got this woman with giant mammaries getting it on with this big loser Neanderthal. It was a real hit for awhile. I think this explains why the French are so horny. But imagine: men have been drooling over those pictures for millennia, until monkey-women got updated into real-life women (BI #52) which are coincidentally much hotter. 'God bless the upright walkers' is what I always say when I wake up in the morning, 'God bless genital hygiene.'

I think it's really great that a woman invented one of the best inventions ever. It's a real score for feminism because women are always complaining how men never let them invent things. Well, move over, Alfred Einstein and Marie Curie, you hornball, because Pernok takes the cake.

I had this one girlfriend who complained that I was 'holding her back' and 'not letting her fulfill her womanly potential.' So I stepped back and was like, 'Hey, do your thing; don't let me get in the way.' Then it turned out she just wanted to have sex with a better looking guy then me, this French guy named Charley. But his name was really pronounced 'Shar-*lay*' with a soft 'c'-'h' which I thought was superwussy. I would have kicked his ass but he was a giant dude, like *massive*. He was rich as shit too because he invented the Neon Popsicle (BI #77). Also he had a robot suit. I couldn't get near the guy.

I was hanging out with Seal for a few months there after my girlfriend dropped my ass. It was nice just to have a warm body around. You can really count on Seal. I even thought about getting him back his robot body because he was so good to me. But that thing's locked up in the CIA these days. You'd have to *have* a robot body just to *steal* that robot body and then I thought 'What's the point?' because, what, like I'm gonna hoard robot bodies or something? 'For chrissakes, man, there's people starving,' I said to myself, 'don't be so selfish.'

I'm personally working on creating an edible computer or an edible CATscanner. I'm not trying to hit #1 and misplace blowjobs or even porn but I would like to make my contribution to the human species. I'd like to at least beat Neon Popsicles. I'm not trying to downplay Shar-*lay*'s contribution, I just think that there's something obvious about Neon Popsicles. Someone would've come up with that eventually. I don't even care that he's French.

So anyway I think I'll hit the head and do some serious thinking. Let's say for instance when you're building a regular computer you could substitute, instead of wires, green beans;

instead of keys, caramel squares; instead of circuits, baked beans; instead of resistors, bacon-flavored baked beans, you'd have a heck of a good invention there. One of the best ever you could even say. Then, when your computer gets old you wouldn't have to throw it out, you could just fry it up with some eggs. Or I could just put eggs in there, instead of the electricity. So you could just fry up your used computer with some butter and eat up. Wait, I'll make the RAM butter. So basically you could just set the computer on fire and have a big meal. But remember to save your porn files on another set of caramel/eggs/green bean/baked beans and mark them carefully. I don't care if you masturbate like god, you show some respect to Pernok, you goddamn blasphemous bastard.

I Would Die for Bon Jovi

Sometimes I sing on the toilet. Sometimes I sing in the shower. Sometimes I sing in the swimming pool. People say I sound like Boy George in his heyday and that makes me feel like Bon Jovi's sister.

Sometimes when I'm happy I pretend I'm Bon Jovi's sister, the younger one not the older one, which is the one I met at an '88 concert though she didn't treat me very nice. She probably thought I was just some regular Bon Jovi fan and she didn't know that I'm BonBon's number one biggest fan on this whole planet I'm practically a member of his family. If she had known that I own all of his trading cards, an airplane meal he half-finished on a flight to Norway before getting sick, not to mention three pairs of his underwear, she probably would have treated me nicer and told me personal things about BonBon that none of his other wannabe fans know, like the names of his childhood imaginary friends, or the age that he *actually* became potty-trained, as opposed to what his website says, which is that he was potty-trained on a train in Southern Italy at the age of four. But everyone knows that while Bon Jovi visited *Northern* Italy at age four with his two aunts, he didn't visit *Southern* Italy until he was eight. I don't know who's writing for that website but they don't really know anything and I sure hope for their sakes that BonBon doesn't catch wind of that mistake because it really might throw off his beautiful singing voice knowing that his fans aren't really appreciating him as a musician. And then you know what will happen? Maybe he'll go hoarse or he won't be able to sing publicly and then I swear I'd kill myself. There would be less beauty in the world all because of some stupid mistake.

I wrote an email to that website correcting the mistake and I said, "Hey people, this is not a joke, let's get that info right. This is Bon Jovi we're talking about."

I started an unofficial Jon Bon Jovi fan club ten years ago and it currently has over 6,000 members. I'm the Founder, President, and Chief of Facts and Information. My cousin is the Finance Officer but not because she cares about Bon Jovi even half as much as I do but because I can't deal with money. I'm always buying Bon Jovi stuff like bedcovers and towels and these cereal spoons with his beautiful face grafted onto the handle. How awesome is that! And I buy things that I think he'll like, like a forest-green riding mower I keep in a shed if he ever visits his unofficial fan club Founder one day because he knows he's always invited. I also bought an old-fashioned art-deco dirt bike with a sidecar that I thought maybe he'd want to ride around one day with me, of course I'd be in the sidecar. Basically, my point is I can't handle money. So my cousin who has an on-line degree in accounting from E-University, because she won some essay contest that Oprah gave about guessing the weight of each of her thighs after she lost weight on some crash diet, and my cousin guessed 42 lbs each, and the real answer was 44 lbs which was really close, much closer than some idiots. One guy even guessed 5 lbs and a different guy guessed 250 lbs. For a thigh? What an idiot! We were all laughing about it with Oprah the other day at four p.m. when her show's on but in the end my cousin won this voucher for E-University and now she's a licensed accountant so she keeps an eye on my spending habits.

I'm still always sending Bon Jovi stuff by mail, like pictures of the riding mower that I keep in the shed, or me in a bikini in his dirt bike sidecar. I sent him by FedEx this really cool toaster from Target that opens from the top because I know how he likes his toast just the perfect way, and I also sent him a book about having good sex in your middle age. That's a joke between me and him because of course he doesn't need advice about sex and also it hasn't been proven that he ever ages. Anyway, the book didn't even get to him, about half of the stuff I send gets sent back. Like the toaster came back with half a Poptart shoved into it by some asshole mailman. But every once in a while I'll get a personally signed letter and a snapshot with Bon Jovi's personal stamp. I have 28 snapshots with his personal stamp.

I'm not letting any not-real fans into my fan club anymore because I've found they really ruin it. After a popular album like his last all the kids wanna jump on the trendy train and buy T-shirts and buttons and Jovi-Jackets. But I know they'll only wear them for a week or two until some other star gets an album on the charts like Britney 'Sucky' Spears or Celine 'Sucks-Worse' Dion, and even though those bitches are not half as good as BonBon they are totally deluded. People are such whores it makes me want to throw up. I wear a T-shirt of Bon Jovi's first European tour to bed every night since the age of nine. I would die for Jon Bon Jovi. I hope the day Bon Jovi is going to die, he calls me up so I can die instead of him. Like, if it's a bullet, I'll take that bullet for him or if it's a vicious dog, I'd let that dog tear my throat out to save Bon Jovi's throat. But I might convince my cousin to do it instead. She really hasn't proven her love for BonBon even half as much as me. Plus she could never run Bon Jovi's Unofficial Fan club like I do. That would be like someone trying to be Bon Jovi once Bon Jovi is dead, which is like someone pretending that the world has meaning when it is clearly a dead and lifeless existence.

It's my dream, that even though I'm not pretty, Bon Jovi will make love to me one day. I know that's crazy because for one thing he's married and number two there's a line of beautiful woman from here to Alaska begging to have sex with Bon Jovi. But my thinking is that maybe Bon Jovi will see how much I love him, and I love him, I do. Maybe one day he'll see the light and he'll realize that I've got a lot of talent. Soon I'm going to print my bestseller *Cooking with Toothpaste* and then he'll see I'm special too, special enough for him.

Camp Willpower

Dear Mom and Dad,

    I'm learning a lot about life in camp. Three boys in the bunk are homosexuals and the head counselor kisses us on the mouth before we go to sleep. Why didn't you buy me that goddamn GameCenter like I asked? Jeremy is always talking about how awesome his new GameCenter is and everybody here thinks I'm an asshole.

  -K

Dearest Kenny,

    Me and your Dad gave it some thought and we bought you the new updated GameCenter even though the one you have is only two months old. Your younger brother says that they are exactly the same as far as video systems go except for the box design and the extra disc-holder. But I know you'll enjoy and appreciate, since we trust you to make your own decisions…

  Luv,
  Mom

Mom and Dad,

    Harry doesn't know shit about videogames. I need that extra disc-holder. By the way, I'll kill that fuckface if he touches my new GameCenter. My new bunkmate's name is Sven. He's from Europe or something. I think he's a homo because he'll only change his clothes underneath the sleeping bag. Also he turns red when the girls talk to him. Man, I get such a boner when Melissa talks to me. But there are some real fat gross girls here that look like they only eat vanilla pudding all day. Sven only showers with his bathing suit on. I saw him looking at the hair on my balls and I said 'Hey homo, it's a quarter for the first five minutes.' Pretty good line, huh, Dad?

-Kickass K

Dear Kenny,

Your father is away on a business trip to Cuba but he said he really liked your joke to the foreign boy. Tell me, honey, have you lost any weight yet? You know you're perfect in every way but Camp Willpower really costs a lot of money. Remember how mad you got when Charley said you have a bosom like Aunt Carol? He'd goose you less, if there was less to goose. Plus, I want you to look nice for your bar mitzvah suit… I picked out a beautiful shiny blue tie, just like the one your father wore on our first date…

Luv,
Mom

Mom,

Why the fuck are you telling me about your love life? God, I hate when you do that. As if I don't know that you slept with Dad on your first date… Uncle Charley's such a fuckface, Mom. By the way, he said I have man-tits not a bosom. I know he's your brother but I hope he dies. I saw him snorting coke out of Harry's crib when he was a baby. That's why Harry's face is so distorted and he always shits in the pool.

Anyway, I lost like 100 pounds already because the food is so disgusting. I'm getting nervous that the camp nurse is gonna think I'm anorexic so I'm gonna find a way to get some bonbons and pizza in here. I think I can bribe one of the waiters. Seriously, mom, I'm so skinny I'm starting to look like Kate Moss.

I can't believe you sent me here. These kids are so fucking gross and fat, I can't even talk to them, they're pathetic. For lunch, they only have diet fruit punch which tastes like piss. On Tuesdays we get these fishcakes that are gray. I swear they smell like an old vagina.

-Kenny

Dear Kenny,

I did *not* sleep with your father on our first date. We met for lunch in the cafeteria and believe me, it wasn't an option. That second date was the most beautiful because that was the day we put in our application with the stork for our beautiful Kenneth Delilah.

Kenny, me and your father really spent a lot of money on Camp Willpower. The deal was that you get to go on MTV Spring Break if you do what you promised, so I really want you to stick with the program. Your father wanted to use that money to buy a second Miata. You know when you go to the orthodontist your braces are going to cost an arm and a leg, so I hope you appreciate this sacrifice.

Luv,
Mom

Mom,

I told you I disowned my middle name so never use it again or I'll disown you. Hey, send me some of those handheld video games. I gave away all of mine to my new friends. This guy Jeff said he'd hang out with me in New Jersey if I get him the new WatchTower II game. He's a really nice guy and his dad has a shotgun he said I can use. Also he lives on the same block as

Christie Brinkley and she showers with the window open so you can see everything.

Anyway tell Rosalita I need new jeans because I'm so skinny. One pair of each color. If they don't fit she can return them. Tell her to widen the dick-part for me because my dick really grew this summer and I need the room. Listen, Mom, send some condoms. I just want to be safe. There are some real whores here and it might be awesome. I'll let you know.

-Kickass Kenny

Dear Kenny,

I called up the head counselor and he said 12-year-old boys don't need condoms. But I understand that you're almost a man now and I'll get Harris to go through your pornography magazines if you tell me which ones you want. Uncle Charley moved into our pool house again. It's only on condition that he not make fun of you when you get back from camp. Also, I asked him about the cocaine-habit that you mentioned and he denied it. He's my brother so I feel I should give him the benefit of the doubt.

Dear, I don't mean to pick a fight or be disbelieving, but there will be a lot less potential jokes for Charles to make if you *really* do slim down like you promised. Charles has always been thin like all the members of my side of the family. Harris, too. Dear, you have to know that it's hard for us to understand heavy people like you and your father.

Honey, I'm going to let Harris use the skateboard we gave you for Christmas. I know you hate sharing but Harris has been a really good boy—he cleaned out the garage which is something you promised to do six months ago. Plus, you've never used the skateboard even once.

Luv,
Mom

Mom,

Don't let Fuckface into my room or I'll stab him. I was gonna clean the garage the second I got back from camp. Why are you always blaming me every second? I knew that Harrison would spend all summer kissing your ass. He only cleans stuff to make me look bad. I don't want him touching any of my shit because he's gonna fuck everything up.

That skateboard was signed by Tony Hawkes who is the world's greatest skateboarder which is something you and Harris don't know about. It's a collector item which is why I don't use it. That's like using your diamond earrings every day. What the fuck! And my porno mags are carefully organized. I don't keep the softcore in the same place as the hardcore anymore and Harris won't be able to find anything. Rosalita knows which girls I like best because she walks in on me jerking off all the time. She always stares at my dick and afterwards I think she steals some of my underwear. She probably takes it home and dreams about me.

Mom, I don't think you're thin by the way, more like bony. When Charley wakes up and hasn't showered he looks like a crazy homeless skeleton. He lives on sangria. People think me and Dad are fat but we're both really strong. Hey, how come Dad never wrote me yet?

By the way, did you know that Rosalita tried to have sex with me once? It's true. She showed me all these pictures of her kids that she keeps in her wallet and she was like breathing all over me and then she was crying and then she hugged me. God her tits are so big. I think we should fire her after she finds those pornos I like.

-Kenny

Dear Kenny,
We can't fire Rosalita! I don't know what I would do without

her, I'd just about die. For instance, yesterday we had a dinner party for the gold members at the country club and we were one plate shy of shrimp. I thought I would commit suicide but Rosalita kept her head. She brought me two valiums and a white wine to calm me down. Then she shared the fifteen platters into sixteen. Isn't that clever? The party was saved…The real problem was that Mr. Kendricks brought his wife *and* his girlfriend. How tacky! Not that I mind one way or the other about his personal life but for godsakes let a hostess know beforehand. Then old Mrs. Caroline got plastered and did a number two in the bidet… she takes so many pills that even one glass of wine makes her loony as a homeless person. She almost stripped down to her bloomers and girdle during dessert. Thank god for Rosalita. She scooped up Mrs. Caroline's ass and boobs, shoved them in a cab, and then had the bidet looking new in two minutes flat…

    Luv,
    Mom

Mom,

    Thanks for the really gross image of Mrs. Caroline naked taking a dump. What is she, like 100 years old? I can't even look at these pornos now.

    Today we went canoeing and I almost drowned. Some fuckhead girl smashed me with a paddle and nobody checked that my lifejacket has a weight limit. It was kinda cool at the end because the canoeing lifeguard lady was leaning over me and I could see her cleavage. Then she made a joke and said I have 'boobs' and we felt each other up. Seriously, send me condoms because she is horn-*ay* for me. Dad told me to get laid in camp and I don't want to let him down. The canoeing company said from now on I have to use two life jackets tied together.

    -Kenny

Kenny,

    Your Dad ran away to Jamaica with his secretary, you know the one, she's got big teeth and shakes her ass whenever she walks by his desk, Camilla or Chamomile or Chlamydia or whatever. I should have seen this coming. I could smell whore-husband-stealer on that bitch from a mile away. So anyway don't expect any letters from dear old Dad anytime soon unless it's a postcard saying he doesn't give a shit about anyone but his fat scumbag self. You see what happens? I never tell any of you what to do. I talked to Leon, this lawyer I've been seeing for eight months, and he's sure we can take him to the cleaners. That fucker's gonna bleed cash...

-Mom

Mom,

    Do you at least have Dad's address in Jamaica? I need to ask him about surfing lessons when I get back. Maybe I can visit them at their beach house... I really don't think you should be so hard on the guy. He's a really important lawyer and he told me before I came to Camp Willpower that you guys weren't having sex since Harry was born. Maybe if you begged Dad to take you back or baked him a cake or something. He probably just went to Jamaica for a short vacation.

Love,
Kenny

Kenny,
You're going to have to find your way home from camp yourself. Charles checked me in to a substance abuse center. I'll take any pill in the damn world so long as I can wash it down with some white wine. Rosalita will be here when you get home.

-Marion

Father Knows Best

    Remember when you were in the shower right up to the part of the shower where you wash your armpits and a green cop car pulled up onto the front lawn and started blaring its siren. Then the cop pulled out a megaphone and was like, 'Come out with your hands up!' And you were totally befuddled because usually when the time comes during the shower for your armpits to get clean, they do so without much complication. But then the cop stopped talking politely into the megaphone, and started yelling instead which multiplied the volume level so considerably that the jelly of your thighs jiggled and the showersoap could not be applied evenly.

    Remember how you hate being yelled at in the shower which is why in the first place you disowned your family so your armpits and thighs could get clean without a whole lot of hullabaloo, what with your daughter always yelling at you to stop singing and your wife laughing at you naked and your son always flushing the toilet so the water turns ice cold and your dick retracts like a turtle's head in an ice storm. But that green cop didn't know or didn't care about your preference for shower solitude because there he was on your lawn yelling holy hell.

    Remember how you went outside with the soap in your hand and the towel wrapped not quite as tightly as you normally like around your waist and the cop yelled into the bullhorn,

'Immediately stop and go back inside and put on some clothes,' and you were like, 'I locked myself out,' which totally sucked because you're usually pretty good about remembering your house keys. But this time you forgot, not at all because of your own fault, and now, outside, there was a steadily growing crowd of neighbors and former family members.

Remember how the girl who used to be your daughter was like, 'Daddy got fat,' and you remembered once again why you disowned her especially of all. Then the cop—even louder—was like, 'Go back inside immediately, you are disgusting,' and you were like, 'I can't,' and the cop was like, 'We're gonna shoot you, fatpig, if you don't put your hands down now and go inside,' and you started sniveling and were like, 'Please, Mister Greencop, don't shoot me for being fat I forgot my key,' and a little boy came through the crowd and was like, 'Don't shoot my fat daddy,' and you got real angry, real fast, and turned to the little boy and were like, 'You set this up, you little piece of crap, just so you could interrupt my shower,' and the little boy was like, 'Don't say that, Daddy, I love you and miss you, I don't even care how fat you got or that everyone can see your thingie,' and you started walking towards the crowd to give that little boy a smack on his disrespectable bottom, and the green cop started yelling into the megaphone, 'Do not come over here, go back into the house,' and then, when you were about to grab the kid, the cop had the megaphone right up to your face and was like, 'MOVE BACK FATPIG DADDY!' and pieces of spit were going through the megaphone onto your newly washed face. That really sucked because, on principle, you don't like to take multiple showers on any one day.

Remember how you went to the garden hose and washed your face as a show of protest to the policeman because you didn't think his spittle was particularly clean. Then the green cop turned to the crowd and was like, 'Everybody move back, this fat man won't put on clothes, so everybody's life has got to go on pause while he walks around naked.'

Remember how at that point you really had enough of being called fat, six times being the upper limit of your tolerance. So you decided to borrow the extra key from the next door neighbors, the McArgles, to get back inside the house. Man, did Mrs. McArgle take a long gander at that flimsy towel as she dangled that extra key. Remember you were like, 'Enjoy it up close, old bag. I know you peek into my bedroom window with your opera glasses,' and she gasped and ran inside, probably to hide her opera glasses and masturbation jelly, or whatever she uses when she checks you out. She probably got nervous about the green cop on the front lawn, that he might have a supernatural talent for nosing out old lady pervs, even though you knew he was just a forest ranger.

Then remember you took the extra front door key and were about to get inside the house when your disowned wife tapped the cop on the shoulder and was like, 'If my husband goes inside he'll sneak out the back window,' and the cop shouted into the megaphone: 'Stop right there and put your hands up.' You couldn't believe that woman, the mother of your ex-children, could have ratted you out like that, but you considered that perhaps it was your own fault. You thought: 'Damn that woman, I shouldn't have jumped out of the 'Just Married' car window after our wedding. She got wise to my tricks. Plus I never took advantage of all those chances to smother her sleeping face.'

Remember how Mr. McArgle came over from next door and stole back the garbage can that you had stolen last winter. He huffed at you and pointed to the name on the garbage can which was clearly labeled 'The McArgle's,' as if the problem all along was not that you were an outright thief, which you are, but that you hadn't understood the writing on the side of the garbage can.

Remember how you decided, right then and there, that when you got out of this naked-on-the-front-lawn mess, you would throw McArgle and his perv wife into that garbage can chopped into bologna bits. But clearly at this point you were overwhelmed. More green cops had shown up as backup to the first green cop, and the woman you had once called your wife was showing the first green cop your driver's license and birth certificate, heaven knows how she got her hands on them. Your ex-daughter, too, was leafing through an old photo album and explaining to the neighbors how you hadn't always been so fat. 'Look,' she said, 'here he is at Chuck E. Cheese where he used to eat only two slices. Now he'll eat a whole pie by himself.' Then the boy who used to be your son added his two cents, 'After a while he wouldn't even take us anymore, he just went to Chuck E. Cheese alone to play in the colored balls. What a bad father…'

Well, you put your hands up because the pressure had gotten too much. 'I'm not your father,' you told that orphan boy for the hundredth time.

'I'm not related to any of these people,' you insisted to the green cop, hoping to gain a measure of his sympathy. 'Look how they molest me during quiet time.' Of course, by this time, after all the excitement, the towel had gotten pretty loose and with your hands lifted, it fell down right there on the frontlawn pathway, and you showed your goodies to a whole block of fairly respectable suburban folks. The cop was like, 'Pick up your towel immediately' and while you bent down to pick it up, he was like, 'Good lord, not that way,' but it was too late. Everyone caught a glimpse of the drugs you were hiding in your ass.

Here's the moral of the story: Always remember to take the drugs out of your ass before a shower if you're a mule for a Mexican drug cartel because, otherwise man, you'll get busted every time. Quite honestly, you had no reason to lollygag other than thoughtlessness. All your buddies in the drug cartel warned you not to trust your family, even if you disown them. They said: chop them up and put them in the neighbors' garbage can. But it's too late now.

Good God, you might never have a quiet shower again.

Future future

Twenty years ago when people were like cyberlink-this and ethernet-that, everyone else was like "Holy shit is that guy from the future?" But I knew all along that shit would be passé in about five seconds. Now when I go up to chicks and I'm like "Do you want to ride on my magnetic hovercraft?," they're like "Are you from the future future?" And I'm like "Hell yeah and I've got special fuck techniques that won't be available to the human race for another forty years." And they're like totally immersed in what I'm saying, trying to give me their email addresses but they don't know that I'm past email, man, that shit is for posers. Then just to tease them I'm like, "Have you ever heard of the *Bifurcated Andromeda Poontang*?" and they're like, "No," and I'm like, "Of course not, it's from the alien galaxy Grobo, which is a virtual Universe that is eleven millenium old, so how could you ever hear of it using your pathetic communication satellites which can barely talk to anything outside of the Earth's ozone?" And they start whining because they really want to know what my secret word means so I tell them it's a sex move which is probably the most pleasurable feeling that any being could experience... By then there's usually a group of really good looking girls standing around and trying to get a hand inside my all-polyester silversuit which is signed by Captain Kirk and Captain Picard (hell yeah!) and they're like, "Oh my god that sounds sexy, please do it to me," and I'm like, "It's not really a sex move. That's simplistic earth-thinking that you're still using. It's more of an extended yoga meditative superfuck in a medieval Russian tearoom. Sex is not really cool anymore on planet Grobo. Some of the old people do it but the young ones kinda make fun of them behind their backs."

Then the girls start getting whiny and maybe trying out the *Bifurcated Andromeda Poontang* on their own, as if they would have a chance of getting it right. I always try to stop them so that they don't accidentally kill themselves. Not that it's my business one way or the other, but I can't let them die. The planet Grobo is extremely Grobian which is like the same as humanistic except times one million. Basically, if even one Grobon dies, then the sex on Grobo gets worse. Isn't that crazy! That would be like if your mother died and, consequently, having sex with your wife got worse.

The Mother

She doesn't like closed doors! But I do. A man needs privacy and more than that. Anything to get away from those always-watching eyes. She doesn't trust anybody or anything! Haughty like a Chinese princess, The Mother never blinks. In my short time on this planet I've learned one thing: never cross The Mother.

I got nerves, let me tell you. Like a war veteran or dope fiend though I've never been in a war or done drugs. Sometimes I feel like I'm gonna break apart. I start trembling and something's upon me, a chill, a ghost, some involved darkness. Then I gotta get the phonebook and phone somebody to talk nice to me as I smoke a cigarette and calm down.

"Oil that hinge," she says, but some doors you like squeaky. It's too easy for her to kill. If only the graveyard wasn't so close… she could dispose of the evidence in two trips. Even the body as deadweight would pose no challenge. I barely weigh one hundred pounds as it is. It's all I can do to waste away.

She caught me last week.

"Why are you here?" It was three a.m. and she waved a glittering butcher knife in the unlit kitchen.

"I was afraid the snack foods would go bad."

"Stop lying and get to your room. I thought you were a burglar. If you keep ruining your appetite I'll stop cooking for you…"

What she scrapes from the washroom tiles she calls cooking? Everyday I'm slowly poisoned by bathtub scum. The contraband potato chips I eat are all that sustain my fragile soul. But she doesn't mind. The less I weigh, the smoother the crime. That long butcher knife yearns for separating meat. Without the head, I'm barely eighty pounds. Without the arms and legs, not forty. She could make two trips and feed the rest to the dogs.

I learned on my ninth day that the door locks were purely aesthetic. "I don't like secrets," she said. It was the fifteenth day before I was brave enough to mention my consternation. Subtextually, I did so: "A man of my condition requires four silent walls."

Never could I admit straightforwardness in my present state. I am sick, you see, sick in the head, committed to that sickness, intent on being committed. But I can't remember if I went mad before I got here or afterwards. If The Mother was the one who made me lose my mind then I had better leave. What new madness might come on the tail of this present insanity? Oh no, even one degree more and I'll tear my eyes from my head. Even now, on nights I think I might die in my sleep I keep a phone by the bedside. Before I close my eyes at night I punch in the "nine" and the "one" and then I know, if something comes upon me, some sudden death, if I should choke on some vomit of fear, I can press that final "one" and at least some police tape-machine can record my last moments.

On the other hand, if I was mad before The Mother found me, I had certainly better stay. That seems reasonable. A crazy person has no place in workaday society. I might very well be a basement monster of depraved behavior. She says "I know you'll prey on Catholic-skirts." I admit the thought hadn't crossed my mind but the suggestion carries insinuation. How can a man know if he can be trusted if he can't trust himself? Maybe I *am* a predator. I'd certainly never let a daughter of mine near someone like myself. She says, "If you don't recognize your own leanings, then you're *sure* trouble." My vantage point being what it is, I don't feel I can devise a convincing counter-argument.

One night, not too long ago, the ghosts of death swooned from the ceiling shadows to lick my throat in mockery. I spent the darkest midnight hours puking until my eyes bled tears and my throat swelled shut. I was sure Hell's dawn had flowered upon me and I jumped to the phone. Without my glasses I smashed all the buttons. By the time I found my glasses the feeling had passed, I saw that I was alive, no end was immediate. When I finally got settled, I sat on the bed thinking: "Have I not earned my stripes? No one was there to comfort me when my throat swelled shut from vomiting."

Then, because of the agitation, the knife I keep on the shelf above my bed—the one I wave at the demon-ghosts The Mother sends through the vents—fell down and nicked the edge of my glasses. To me that's a sign if there ever was one. It scared the fear of the Lord into me. Not belief in the Lord, but fear. If He's there I do what he says. If He's not there I do what he says.

I immediately called the police. "Hello" some policewoman said, the voice high-pitched and mechanical. I couldn't believe it was a human voice, "…what's the emergency?"

"I almost died. The Mother hunts me as I escape the teenage girls. It's not my fault they're biologically prepared to have babies."

"Sir, do you want an ambulance to drive by?"

"I'm not going to the hospital, no way. The last time I was at the hospital I watched an infant the size of a tree-squirrel get an IV in its puny arm and it broke my skull. My heart can't witness the genuinely ill. A bleeding heart, that's my true sickness. No germ or cut could ever scare so much."

"Sir, I need this line free for people with emergencies. I can give you a psychology hotline number if you want."

"No, no, The Mother hears all."

After she hung up I called The Mother using the tincan-phone

I keep in the closet.

"Go to sleep," she said, "All that sugary junk food is keeping you awake."

She thinks she knows all, that she can woo me to passivity. But I know there's always a new emasculation waiting after the present one.

"So what if I end up a loveless sack of bones? Who cares that the mortician rapes my body or dances me around his shop with an old woman's dress and hat. There's no dignity for a corpse."

Kokey Pop

It was late April, and Jackie opened the door for Joey's wheelbarrow of ice at six in the morning. Over Jackie's enormous belly stretched a grease-stained, yellow-armpitted undershirt. Aunt Vivian emerged from the kitchen with a hair net over her short perm and watched Joey unpack his ice into the freezer. She said in her coarse, overly-intimate voice, "Even though you're an Italian I can see that you're a good worker who stays out of trouble."

She offered him a job that day doing small chores like moving boxes, taking out the trash, or running to the grocery store. Joey immediately accepted. Uncle Dominick often forgot to pay him on payday and Joey was too shy to complain. He did not even tell Uncle Dominick that he was quitting but simply returned the wheelbarrow into plain view by the warehouse.

Aunt Vivian liked Joey because he was a naturally friendly boy, perfect for a soda-jerk in a small town like Auggsville, West Virginia. Jackie liked the boy because he kept his business to himself. On the outside, Aunt Vivian and Jackie were full of rosy banter and treated the customers like family. But there were rats behind Aunt Vivian's food counter. And Jackie didn't even bother to crush the roaches in the kitchen any longer; they moved about as if they were invited guests. After closing, Jackie and Aunt Vivian would sip rum and lisp curses at each other in the back room of *Aunt Vivian's Diner*. They loved to gossip about the people of Auggsville. One time, Joey overheard them arguing about Jackie's visit to a prostitute. The prostitute was the sister of one of Joey's classmates. Joey kept silent as he worked and when his cleaning was complete, he crept from the Diner without diverting their attention.

As soon as Kokey Pop hit Auggsville that summer, Aunt Vivian promoted Joey to the newly-installed soda fountain. It was a craze. Soda fountains serving Kokey Pop started up all over America; silver faucets and brass spigots and copper levers, everything modern and eye-hurting shiny. Joey kept his work area spotless, and anyone could see that he was glad to do his job right.

Joey wasn't much to look at behind the counter—short and so extraordinarily thin that his service cap sat askew on his head like a lamp on a lamppost that had been hit by a truck. But he was clever and polite to all customers and could be trusted to work without supervision. On his first day at the fountain, Aunt Vivian put him in charge of serving banana splits, Kokey Pop ice cream floats, and Aunt Vivian's famous milkshakes. But Joey found by the second day that he was exclusively serving Kokey Pop.

Something was special about Kokey Pop, there was no doubt. Nothing was more satisfying to Joey than when the bottle opener clicked against the top of a cold bottle. Ice chips slid down its shapely side and the cap popped off with a hiss as if to say: This is a fresh and refreshing product. A world of good taste has been sealed inside for one person alone: You! Now, like a magic genie's lamp, it's open!

And Kokey Pop Incorporated refused to share their secret ingredient. There was much discussion in Auggsville about what *7Z* could be. Some thought it was cinnamon extract, some thought it was nutmeg.

Joey made twenty cents a week and was allowed to serve himself one free Kokey Pop every night once the shop was closed and cleaned up. This was good money for a fourteen-year old boy and Joey always gave half to his mother. Another nickel, like his mother advised, went towards his future wedding. According to her, Joey's father had been killed in a train wreck five years earlier. Uncle Dominick did not indicate that Mama's story matched up—something about Papa's attraction to dice—but Joey did not push for information. A good boy, according to his mother, did not ask questions of the dead.

Secretly, Joey loved the uniform most: the starched white apron and the pointy hat. While his mother gladly offered to wash it every week, she never scrubbed it to a bright healthy white or starched it like Joey preferred. He washed his uniform every evening at seven after he returned home from work. Before he went out to meet his friends, he would hang his ironed uniform to dry so that it would be ready the next afternoon. He only felt comfortable around the sparkling silver spigots, faucets and gleaming countertop of the soda fountain when his uniform matched its cheery brightness, even though the rest of Aunt Vivian's was unclean. He felt that the uniform made an impression on the pretty high school girls who would otherwise ignore him all year round.

It was a good job in all respects except for Friday nights, when Aunt Vivian's stayed open late and the swarms of noisy kids, all on summer break, descended like rats and roaches to cause trouble. If a group of boys spotted a group of girls the scene would turn instantly rowdy. Jackie and Aunt Vivian would curse under their breath at the immigrant kids and Joey would keep silent. He was ashamed at his friends for acting so childish but he was also jealous because he could never let go like *that*, like a regular teenager.

Especially when he saw Marisa he wished so badly to perform correctly and make clever jokes. Marisa was a cheerleader and the prettiest girl in high school. She usually arrived at Aunt Vivian's holding hands with Chad the quarterback and the store would quiet for Auggsville's royal couple. Marisa looked so petite to Joey, so lively and desirable in her pleated cheerleader skirt and bobby socks, that her arrival made Aunt Vivian's feel to him warmer than church. But Marisa only occasionally acted friendly to him, and whenever he approached with a Kokey Pop order, one of her cheerleader friends would undoubtedly make a snide remark towards the wimpy soda jerk. Whenever the upperclassmen were reminded that Joey was a freshman they would give him trouble; trip him in the aisle, ignore the bill, spill drinks on his uniform. Joey felt best when he was quietly serving Kokey Pop and ice cream from behind the counter because he knew he did that well.

After hours, when all the kids had gone home and Jackie had had a few drinks, he told Joey, "Don't take that gump, kid. Give 'em hell." But Joey was small, not even arrived at puberty yet and he didn't want trouble.

After a month of Kokey Pop's arrival, the soft drink started getting so popular that Jackie began helping Joey behind the soda fountain. Then the two Eastern-European girls from the kitchen began assisting. Soon, Aunt Vivian joined too. Barely anyone wanted Aunt Vivian's food anymore—even her famous Thousand-Island-Hamburger or Key Lime Pie. Nobody was interested in anything but Kokey Pop.

Throughout the day, customers climbed into Joey's face and pushed each other at the countertop grabbing for a glass. Even the adults acted wild. At least one fight erupted everyday. Officer Seaver began watching from the corner booth, patiently sipping Kokey Pops. Aunt Vivian ordered six times the amount of Kokey Pop as before and still ran out before the week was up. After two weeks of frenzy, Aunt Vivian decided to stop serving it altogether.

"It's too much trouble," she said, "I think it's too sweet anyway." She ordered a different brand called Proppers Cream.

The heavy customer traffic quickly died down and Officer Seaver left, too. Throughout the next day customers stopped in and asked for Kokey Pop:

"C'mon kid. Maybe you got an extra one in the back. Why dontcha go check? Goddamnit just go and check willya…"

After hearing of the change, the customer might try a Proppers Cream. But they always left the Diner slumped and disappointed. Aunt Vivian and Jackie went back to serving greasy lunch food to regular customers, mostly the workers from the mattress factory down the road. Some of the high school kids came weeks later begging for a Kokey Pop even when they knew very well that Aunt Vivian's only served Proppers bottles.

Joey, too, was getting headaches. He desperately missed his daily Kokey Pop. One day, just as Joey was cleaning off the counter top, Marisa came in holding her head. Her cheerleader uniform was dirty and unkempt. She sat down on a stool and pouted her lips at Joey.

"Hey Marisa, what can I get you?"

He approached and found that Marisa smelled like a sewer.

"Hey, little man. I'll take one Kokey Pop."

"We're all out. We haven't served it for weeks now."

"Oh God… you don't have *one*?" she pouted her lips and squirmed on the stool, "I saved up a whole case but I drank it all. I need a Kokey Pop, kid. Help me out…"

"I'm sorry, M-M-Marisa, we're all out. Do you want a Proppers Cream? With ice cream?"

"Oh C'mon…" she played with his name tag, "Joe. Joey. Joe-Joe. I know you got one more. Maybe one in the back. Maybe half of one…" Her shoulders shook. Bits of spittle collected at her lipcorners.

Joey took a step away and shook his head. "I'm sorry. Nothing's left."

Kokey Pop

"… Don't hold out on me, little man." She moaned and twisted her body so that her uniform raised and Joey could see a slip of bare skin. "C'mon, I'll let you feel me up. I'll let you do what ever you want…" She reached over the countertop and grabbed his uniform, "Goddamnit, kid… Get me a Kokey Pop!"

Joey felt sick. He had goosebumps all over his body. "It's illegal. They made it illegal. We don't serve it anymore. No one does."

"Oh *no*! Oh no." She started weeping uncontrollably and collapsed her head onto the counter. "No no no."

After ten minutes, the weeping died down. Joey asked, "Are you OK?"

Marisa looked to the out-of-use Kokey Pop dispenser.

"Joey. I'm just gonna take a chance..." Marisa climbed over the counter, put her lips to the soda fountain spout and sucked. She smashed her hand on the counter and began tearing.

"Nothing… goddamnit… goddamnit…"

She lifted her head with a crazed look in her eyes and darted from the store. Joey was speechless; she looked like a rat searching for cover. Joey watched her pause outside Aunt Vivian's front window to fix her lips and hair before scampering off.

Baby License

Cameron spikes the baby. He kicks it skidding across the kitchen floor. He doesn't want a baby; he never did. He hates being interrupted from TV watching, he hates sharing his food and time. All in all, he knows himself as a selfish man, unregretful of this selfishness. He smashes a fist into its face, into its belly. The throat emits a scattered shrill alarm, *Kee-wikee-kee* until Cameron yanks out the embedded noisemaker. The crying stops but the jaw keeps working, up and down, with a regular, mechanical drone. Cameron takes a screwdriver from the tool drawer and pries the tip against the baby's tongue. The jaw pops off. He peels away at the facial plastic skin. He stabs out both of the glass eyes and, like a madman possessed, starts to work away at the hairline; a minuscule rise is used to lever off the skull. Suddenly, as if in a dream, the sound of his wife's car pulling into the driveway reaches his ears.

Instinctively, he throws the baby into the garbage bin and scoops a handful of scattered babyparts from the floor. He drapes a newspaper over it. He notices a burn-smell lingering, but before he can run to the sink for air freshener, his wife walks in.

"Hey, honey."

He responds breathlessly and kicks the excess mess onto the living room carpet, covering his tracks. As she walks into the kitchen he moves boldly to hug her. In an embrace, he leans over to the wall console and flips the stove fan switch.

"What are you doing?" she asks.

"What do you mean?" he holds her tightly and she struggles to free herself. A look of panic crosses her face.

"What's wrong with you?"

"Nothing. Nothing's wrong." He shrugs, attempting to look casual. As his newlywed wife looks him over, he realizes he is sweating and unkempt. His shirt is untucked from his suit pants and there is ash and dirt all over his brown suit jacket.

"Where's the baby?" She steps towards the garbage can.

"Listen," he grabs her shoulder, roughly spinning her, "I don't want you to get mad."

"Oh!" she yanks her arm away. She understands he has done something rash and her heart rebels. When he gets wild like this, like a drunk frat-brother, she is instantly transported to sorority days. His bouts of mania bring sex and danger equally to mind.

"What the fuck!" Visions of lovemaking occupied her mind, warming her, on the car ride home. She forces herself away from traitorous thoughts. She knows Cameron's anger must be checked or else, she too will grow shrewd and cagey like her intoxicated college days. She knows how easily she could abandon her job, rupture her life. She stares at him, stares him down, until his eyes guiltily flick towards the garbage can. She steps hesitantly away, never turning her back.

"Christy. Wait..."

Now she is near the garbage bin. She hears a grinding sound. She looks down and sees the baby, what is left of it, face down, the motor of its legs grinding persistently, kicking in futile circles. Its arms are torn off. She lifts it up and looks down the red hole of its gaping throat.

"Oh my God!" She is more flabbergasted than frightened. She cannot excuse such an attack in her own home, even to a lifeless dummy. The IRB will never remove the birth-control patch from her arm.

"I can't do it, Christy. The thing was wailing when I came in from work and I couldn't take it. Borheimer wouldn't take my report and then he took credit for my program on Abatex that *I've* been working on for two weeks. When I walked in the door I just—"

"You–crazy–fucked–up–asshole!"

"—I was just crazy when I came in." Cameron puts his palms against his forehead to dramatize, "I couldn't take it and maybe it's for the best, you know what I'm saying. I don't think I'm ready for that thing."

She turns the baby in her hands and inspects the brutal damage. "Oh, my God." She looks in wonder at her husband standing in defeat, guilty for taking it out on a defenseless toy. She can scarcely fathom the fury which accompanied the attack. She knows, suddenly, there was insanity involved. At this moment, however, in his disheveled suit, his arms flung wide and pleading, he looks at her with frank-eyed innocence. She begins laughing and laughs uproariously until she is teary-eyed and coughing. Her husband watches her with flickering eyes, his guilt transforming into wicked amusement. His wife is strange, a beautiful and unpredictable creature: always wanting one thing, then wanting the complete opposite.

He takes her into his arms, "I'm sorry, you know."

She bats his chest, "You asshole, now we'll never get a real baby."

"Ow. Don't call me an asshole. I didn't know what to do."

She thrusts the baby in front of his face, "We can't bring this to the agency. We'll never get a license. It's hideous."

"Maybe it's for the best."

"No," she pushes away from him, "we're *gonna* get that license and we're *gonna* get a baby."

He sighs and collapses into a chair. She lets him wallow for ten minutes while she readies dinner. When the food is prepared he is still sitting at the table—dazed, pathetic, unattractive—like her weak-blooded father. The sight drives away all warmth.

"I want a baby!" she screams, "I want that license!" She stomps into the bedroom. For the rest of the evening, she refuses to speak. When he enters the bedroom later she is already sleeping.

In the morning, the air is sour and unsettled. Cameron feels her disapproval as a tangible object. Like a hangover, he feels like a bloated and bulky animal, prickly towards other beings, wanting to stay in bed forever. Christy is silent and quiet in her movements. She breezes in and out of the bathroom before Cameron manages a "Good Morning." He asks if she wants a ride to work but she ignores him.

In the shower, he decides on a resolution. Work today with Borheimer will be hell; he will need all his strength not to start a fight. He needs peace at home.

"I'll get a different one."

His voice is moderated with apology. She puts one earring in, then the other. She is wearing the beige business suit that her mother bought as a college graduation gift.

"How?"

"I'll figure it out."

"Hmm. You can't just get another model. They're going to wonder what happened to the first one."

"I'll *get* one. Don't worry."

"Fine." Her mood brightens considerably and she kisses him on the cheek on the way to the bus.

All day, Cameron works diligently. He responds to Borheimer's directions, pushing away indignation, dispelling tension. At lunch he drives to the Infant Registration Bureau. He walks around the building. He feels embarrassed under the gaze of the ten-year-old girls, lined up to the building's back entrance for involuntary birth control installation. They look scared and guilty. In the parking lot, there is a forgotten baby carriage with a Trial-Baby in it. No adults in sight.

Cameron gets behind the baby carriage and begins pushing. He considers taking it to his car but a lady soon exits the IRB sliding doors. She is vigilant in her posture as if looking for something. Cameron pushes the baby carriage towards her.

"Ma'am, I found your baby," he calls. The lady jogs the last few yards between them. She is carrying a real baby in her left arm.

"Oh, thank you!" She is relieved—so dramatically relieved, in fact—that it strikes Cameron as insincere. She takes the Trial-Baby out of the carriage and cradles it in her free arm.

"You must be a father." She looks him over and Cameron can tell she likes him. He is a handsome man in a dirty suit; he looks run-down like a young parent.

"Well, me and my wife have been thinking about it. I was considering getting a Trial-Baby for practice."

"You can have mine." She holds out the Trial-Baby. "I've gotten really attached to it but now we got a real one. Robbie." She holds the real baby forward. He coos dopily. His eyes are glassy from IRB medic-formula.

"I forgot to give it back. I was so excited when I got permission to have a real one. Robbie is the love of my life." Her eyes adopt the same vacant shine of the baby.

"He's a cute kid."

"Thanks. I'm getting confused having both of these around. They look so alike." She is holding the Trial-Baby by one haunch. She waves its head towards Cameron. "Go ahead…"

Cameron takes the Trial-Baby. It is similar in size to the original. It looks cut from the same mold, in fact, except the hair and eyes are darker. He thinks: *Christy will be happy*. The Trial-

Baby begins to squirm in his hands. Robbie reaches a curious hand to touch.

"It needs to be changed, you can tell. You need to change it soon. It makes different sorts of sounds." Cameron holds the Trial-Baby away from his clothes, a hand under each armpit. He checks his suit for stains. The woman giggles.

"Got it. Thank you ma'am. I probably have to clear it inside… with the Bureau?"

"Oh, I don't think so, they're so overworked as it is. I think if you take care of that one, they'll certainly give you the license. A nice man like you. You're a born father, I can see."

"Thank you, ma'am."

Cameron returns home. The new baby is bright red and thrashing wildly. He gives it to Christy.

"Oh, my baby," she coos.

"It needed to be changed an hour ago but I didn't have a diaper."

She gives Cameron a glance and goes back to tickling the Trial-Baby's tummy, "Who needs a change? Wittle baby?"

Later, Christy glows with happiness. She makes love twice to Cameron and falls into deep sleep. At 1 am, Cameron climbs out of bed and heads towards the baby's room.

The Trial-Baby is sleeping soundly. He grabs it by the haunch, dangles it upside-down before his face. He inspects the bottom of its foot as he carries it to the kitchen. The baby struggles and cries. Cameron ties a dishrag across its mouth so it will not wake his wife. He pins it squarely on the kitchen counter and pries the ID tag from its foot. Its eyes turn apoplectic. He heats a soldering iron and briskly grafts the metal ID tag from the first Trial-Baby onto the sole. Under the heat of the iron the baby twists with pain.

"It'll be over in a second, baby. You just be good."

Cameron climbs into bed, the job completed, all loose ends tied-up. Christy drapes a hand over his chest, "Everything OK?"

"Just checking on the baby. Gotta get that license, right?"

"A natural father." She kisses Cameron on the cheek and they make love again before sleep.

Breakfast Sex

    My friend Ethan has a crack cocaine problem. He thinks crack cocaine is the cat's meow, the bombastic fantastic wow-o-rama, the greatest thing since sliced bread only better because bread doesn't get you stoned unless it's crack bread. And guess what, there's no such thing as crack bread because those assholes at Pillsbury don't know a good thing unless it hits them like birdshit in the eye.
    I made up the idea of that squishy little doughboy. On exactly the day of October 6th, Nineteen Hundred and Seventy-Nine, I sat at a barcounter and talked to Captain James Othello Clarkhound who was *then* in the army but is *now* the CEO of Pillsbury, and being that I thought I could trust a military personnel, and besides that having had a few too many drinks, I let my mouth ramble a bit loose and I started talking about how a woman/man made out of dough would be a great ad campaign. The logic behind being fairly obvious in that a sexually ambivalent dough being holds joy for each and every one of us in much the same way as a warm-from-the-microwave cinnamon bun. I even took off my shirt and gave a general demonstration of the dough-body mechanics, of course, giving exception to the fact that I am a generally well-tanned person, artificially perhaps, but nonetheless far from pasty-white. The point being of this story is that I got ripped off, and you might get ripped off too if you don't keep your good

ideas under lock and key. This goes for Aunt Jemima as much as that old Quaker Oats guy, both of whom coincidentally are utterly sexless just like oats and maple syrup gametes. Sex being the last thing you want to be thinking of when you're chowing down on semi-liqueous breakfast grub.

I've seen my good friend Ethan on his hands and knees running his fingers through carpet looking for extra crumbs of crack. He's been in a bad situation, what with his need to feed the beast and it sure was a lesson to me about drug abuse, although it does always strike me as ironic how rich Ethan is, a millionaire since the age of 27. This so-called 'lesson' that I learned while watching a perfectly dignified member of higher society crawl around like a spine-broken slave, was really less useful than one might imagine, because it showed me how little put-together-ness a leader need have. President Bush is a perfect case in point. He smoked pot and so did Clinton. Shit, they probably smoked pot together, them being roommates and all in college. I heard they used to hang out with a mean crowd, all the doors to desirable functions open and inviting, with pretty girls in glittery masks ushering. Sex-parties is what I'm implying, the kind that Joe Blows like me and you can't get into without a waiter jacket. Both these men made it big, there's no bigger than President of These-Here-United-States, even with their brains turned inside out and generally marinated in poison. Mind-*altered*, there's no other way to say it. And that's the kicker, it don't matter a shit one way or the other. Fuck your brain, fuck up the guy next to you, if you've got bank doors open, then your dick is gold and your tongue is silver and the streets are lined with resale electronics.

Fuck, man. That fucker Clarkhound has got what's coming to him. I don't care if he has a million Pillsbury bodyguards and the entire US Air Force satellite division watching his ass, one day he's gonna trip up and someone'll catch him feeling up his landlady in the service elevator. I've seen pictures of Mrs. Captain James Othello Clarkhound. She's got a hairdo like a camouflage shock helmet and a cross-eyed stare that could stop a grenade from exploding. If that guy'll cheat me, he'll sure as hell cheat his glowering half-breed gate-faced wife. Though I don't want to downplay this woman without meeting her. Some of my meanest lays came from ugly chicks, being as they have less shame, less worries about perception of the public eye, whereas hot chicks, though my experience is rare, are more worried that their privates smell like rose bathwater. Etcetera etcetera.

Every time I talk about my sex addiction I can't help thinking of this one prostitute I knew who walked around with a mask made out of sequins which she held up to her face with a stick. She was known as The Red Masque, and an hour with her went progressively up in price as news of her tricks circled my not very large hometown of Care Springs, Pennsylvania. Then the rest of the girls on the block, including the Beverly sisters, started getting masks too in a faddish bandwagon sort of way, people hopping on and off in whim. So the novelty quickly wore off. But it sure started business back up in Care Springs, which used to be a poor excuse for a coal mining town, and is now a poor excuse for a poor excuse for a coal mining town. Economic activity is good in its own way being that people talk more friendly when they're conducting business and otherwise viewing the person across from them as valuable in some way, even the dollar sense. What I'm saying is: more dicksucking means more handshaking means more prayer in the school. What goes around comes around and so forth.

During my town's brief sex craze I got into the get-go of the excitement with my mime act, dressing up and working the street not far from the Beverly girls, two of whom were supportive, while three were not. I took a few mime classes, years ago, under a generally famous Israeli mime named Victor who would make homosexual advances on me despite the fact that he was a voracious carnivore. Traditional heterosexual is what I mean, and he could talk for hours about his *hundreds* of women he had had from all walks of life and modes of social positioning. I always had to beg him to spare the details. He lives a poor and loveless life now, fighting on a grassroots level the fact that he comes across as an old weird dude which is not entirely inaccurate. But he lived the life while he had the chance and you gotta take the low with the high, even though it seems to turn out that the last thirty years of life are the low, decreasing lower.

Naturally I can't portray to you the extent of his miming abilities in a page of writing. It's not that writing lacks the expressiveness of mime, but hell, you lose a lot without the hand gestures. He was *good* is the kicker here. Famous in small internationally-minded artistic circles. I am neither patting myself on the back nor poking fun. I know the limitations of mime as any half-decent mime should. I just bet I have a better grasp than *you*, probability speaking, whoever the fuck you are.

Back to the three-month window sexcraze: I'd be out there on the street in the usual get-up, black stocking shirt, white painted face, white gloves, a bowler hat which upside down sat nice and square on the pavement as if to say, 'I'm a gentleman so give me some cash, you cheap bastard.'

Anyways, a lot of these high school girls, mostly foreign girls like Frenchies, but all one hundred percent legal, don't you worry, they'd come up to me and take me home so long as I did the whole get-go with the makeup on. This was hotshit European-style around which, in the end, I could rarely finish off. Once I was with two of them and I had them trilling like lovestruck Oriole-birds with my rendition of I'm-a-Man-Caught-in-a-Box-and-Pulling-on-a-Cable. Course mine was the updated version: Man-Caught-in-a-Parallel-Universe-and-Pulling-on-a-String-Theory-String. Not that it mattered a whit to those ladies, they were just some fucked-up French chicks who wanted to do the freaky with a circus clown. Those Europeans have grown up drinking sexdrink and eating sexgrub because I can't keep up with them. Not to mention that I was mostly celibate at that time of my life and I only hung out, on principle, with pretty girls bearing noticeable beatific flaws: an eye-patch girl, an attractive harelip, a cripple with hair of extraordinary length and gloss.

Now that I'm open and honest about my sex addiction my life has gotten better. I trademark all my good ideas by sending them certified mail to the President of the United States, even though he's a brainmelted crackface. I figure he doesn't read them, probability speaking, what with his jetting around the world jetset-style, and probing the oceans with expensive Naval equipment for new narcotics made from the marrow of see-through fish, shrimp, and walruses. But he's probably got some underling who's opening up my letters and keeping track of all my miraculous new inventions and abstractions and at least that guy will vouch for me if the time ever comes to sue some idea thief like Captain James Othello Clarkhound or the hybrid breakfast child of the sexless union of Aunt Jemima sitting in a quaking bowl of Mr. Oats' oats.

Evolve, or the World Evolves Without You

PeopleMonkey Meg comes down to breakfast wearing clothes for the first time.

Her brother, PeopleMonkey Sam, prepares himself a bowl of *Banana Crunchies* at the table. "Oh, no," he says, "Look who's so important."

"Shuddup," she replies.

Their father comes in. A loose tie swings from his hairy neck. Still, after two years, he is not comfortable with the company's dress code. He sips his coffee and grunts with mild disapproval when he notices his daughter.

"I'm wearing clothes to school from now on, Dad. I'm paying for it myself."

Her father shrugs and lifts himself from the chair with knuckles planted firmly on the table. He moves sideways into the bathroom.

"You're such a poser. I know you just read *Animal Farm* in class and you want to be like the PeoplePigs wearing clothes and acting like PeoplePeople."

"Nu-uh."

"Yu-huh. You're pathetic. Wannabe!"

"Shuddup," she pours herself a bowl of cereal.

"Pigs are smarter than us anyway."
"No, they're not."
"Yes, they are."
"We ate ham yesterday. How smart could pigs be?"
"So, pigs eat PeopleMonkey."

    In the bathroom, PeopleMonkey Pop sighs and sits on the toilet until his children's voices fade. He stands and sprays his armpits, crotch and mouth with a fragrant concoction which minimizes body-odor. His wife bought it for his birthday. He expects a busy day in the office of picking things up and putting them down. As usual, there will be a lot of sweating.
    He walks past the living room and peeks in. His wife moves along the floor with a vacuum, a new one she just bought, though they have no carpets. She wears a rayon nightgown, a new one, and a satisfied half-smile. When the breeze from the vacuum cleaner seizes her nightgown it appears as though she is swimming through a pool of pearl and silver waves. PeopleMonkey Pop holds his breath. Delicately, hairs from her coat float freely to the ground, ignored by the unplugged vacuum. A patch, now noticeably bald, has been growing on her leg.
    PeopleMonkey Pop ducks his head and shakes away the vision. He is late to work and work is most important. He goes to the kitchen to get his lunch. PeopleMonkey Sam waves a spoon at his sister.
    "Dad, make him stop!"
    "What? I'm not doing anything."
    "Enough," their father grumbles and easily climbs the bottom shelves of the pantry. He begins counting bananas. One. Two. Three. Four… One. Two. Three. Four. Five. Six…
    "Everybody knows you've been practicing every day. *Anyone* can use a handtool if they practice."
    PeopleMonkey Sam dunks his spoon into his cereal and

feeds himself a bite. "So why are you jealous then?"

PeopleMonkey Pop loses concentration. One. Two. Three. Four. He is not a very good counter and he often begins from the beginning multiple times. One. Two. Three. Four. Five. Six. Seven. Eight…

"You know what, *you're* just a show-off like the PeoplePigs."

"Enough!" he yells from the pantry shelf. He feels a headache beginning and the day has barely begun. "One of you get up here and count these bananas for my lunch. Twelve of them."

The children look at each other for a prolonged moment. PeopleMonkey Pop glowers intently—in case they should consider laughing at his poor counting skills.

"Well, I'm not getting my new clothes dirty."

"Now!" he yells. A guttural growl lingers in his throat, truly threatening. Both children visibly tremble. PeopleMonkey Meg looks away; she is more easily scared. Now, she will avoid him for a few days. Pain stabs at his forehead. He can't win, not with fear, not with love. PeopleMonkey Sam rises from his chair and climbs the pantry shelves as his father descends. PeopleMonkey Meg lowers her head to her bowl and takes two last bites.

"Show-off," she says and jumps up. She throws her bowl into the sink and runs out before her brother can complain. PeopleMonkey Sam counts out twelve bananas and puts them on the table in front of his father who has his head on his forearm, eyes closed.

He leans over and watches the breath of his nostrils ruffle his father's shaggy mane. "Mom is losing her fur. The floors are covered with it."

"She'll vacuum it."

PeopleMonkey Pop smiles at his own joke. But then he realizes that his words have revealed something sad, too sad. The vacuum doesn't work. His wife no longer cares to tend to

Evolve, or the World Evolves Without You

household duties or family hygiene in the traditional way. Soon, she will not be his wife anymore. She will be hairless, an unrecognizable creature.

Sam looks at his father's massive skull in this vulnerable position and wants to bite it. "Meg's going to be in the bathroom for an hour now."

His father answers without opening his eyes. "You can go outside like you used to. You're not too good to go outside."

Sam breathes deeply. He thinks: *I could hurt him now.* But he isn't yet strong enough. He knows requital will be excessive. He grimaces and grabs his bookbag, "Forget it, I'll go at school." He runs down the hall and flies outside, slamming the door behind.

The older PeopleMonkey puts his fingers to his temples. He can't figure out what is going on with his kids or his wife. It seems the world is going mad. He can still clearly remember the day when his parents first lowered him from the tree branches to live on the forest floor. He built *this* house with his very own hands and the kids take all of it for granted.

He rises with his bananas. His wife still floats around the living room in her nightgown. She sings a tune to herself, barely audible. When she turns her back to him, PeopleMonkey Pop looks at her critically. He is not sure if she looks ridiculous or beautiful, if he should pick her up or perhaps put her down.

Outside, PeopleMonkey Pop mounts his bicycle and rides north towards work. Thank goodness he has purposefully left a pile of sticks unkempt at the door before the weekend! Now he will have a clear task designated for the whole day. He can duck his head until Tuesday, maybe even Wednesday, before anyone talks to him. That is three days he could go unnoticed.

He hums lightly as he rides. He decides he will yell in the tunnel on the way to work—the long empty stretch beneath the river where no one will hear him, not even strangers. 'Help!' he will yell in the shaded damp darkness and then brush the tears away, swallow it all down. At work, that's the good thing, no one will guess his shame.

Pink Jails

    A book of fiction is assuredly not the ideal forum for a non-fiction piece. Non-fiction is generally boring and uncreative while fiction is pure imagination. What appeals to one appeals to no other. But the suggestion that I wish to offer will only be taken seriously by creative thinkers. It makes sense, *too* much sense, if you know what I mean, so much sense that a non-fiction reader would surely scoff. Fiction readers do not even know how to scoff. If you ask them to scoff, they'll give you a spitty cough, and you'll deserve it too.

    In a nutshell, here is my suggestion: the American government should paint all jails pink. This suggestion probably does not come as a surprise to you if you read the title of this piece which in two words ably sums it up. After you're done with this piece, however, you *will* be surprised because you'll find yourself on the phone to your local politician demanding action about this matter. You'll think: how bizarre that I've never before called this guy up, and it turns out I'm doing it because of *pink jails*.

    Let me ask you, first of all, what you associate with the color pink. Little baby girls? The clothes and dolls of little baby girls? Cotton candy? Marshmallows?

    Now all these pink things are soft and fragile and should be treated gently. Just the mention of them puts me in a placid and blithe state of mind. Gay, even. After all, babies and marshmallows are both wonderful. You surely see where I'm going with this: the ideal state of mind for an American prisoner is placid and gay.

Before you raise any questions, let me address the opposition. 'Catfish,' you say, 'it is well known that American prisons house hardened criminals, some of them psychopathic. What makes you think that they are simple enough to fall for a trick where we paint the prison walls a baby-girlie color? Even American children, without criminal records, will hardly stand still except if a shotgun is pointed at their favorite videogame system.'

Here is the answer: When I walk into a nursery school which is painted wussy colors I feel embarrassed. I want to leave the area as soon as possible. I feel the same in any locale which is painted pink. It makes me feel unmanly. I make a vow never to return to that locale.

Now this is precisely the feeling we should hope to invoke in our inmates. We should want them to feel unmanly in prison (In the sense that they feel ashamed. I don't wish to address the homosexual rape issue at this point). We want them to vow never to return to pink prison, to being treated like a baby girl, even if it means never again performing a crime. Here are some tables of made-up statistics.

American Criminals	hate pink	like pink
male	92%	4%
female	78%	17%

American Criminals	hate rainbows	like rainbows
male	91%	6%
female	81%	15%

I think these tables speak for themselves. We're talking considerable statistical significance. The correlation between

Pink Jails 79

hating the color pink and hating rainbows can and should not be ignored. Rainbow-colored prison-uniforms and all-pink food is where, we as a country, should lead our local politicians. Thank you for your creative time.

The Schizophrenic Mixer

The Schizophrenic Doctors couldn't figure Loretta out. Like many of their patients, she had only three personalities, which remained within their realm of expertise. One of those personalities, however, was Sybil, the notorious 7-personalitied schizophrenic which complicated matters significantly. Loretta either had ten personalities or twenty-three, depending on the mental math. The doctors found themselves outnumbered.

One of the Doctors was afraid Loretta would feel alone in that crowd. He decided to throw her a mixer. "Should we invite all our patients," the other Doctors asked, "or will Loretta just dance with herself?"

Two of the Doctors snorted, but one, a small bald man in a white coat, had a seductive notion: 'Can Loretta self-seduce?' Such possibilities truly enticed: experimentation plus masturbation. 'What would Loretta's personalities exclaim during sex with themselves?' The doctor ran to his office to make manic notes for his Nobel Prize acceptance speech.

The other Doctors took out a sheet of paper and began to plan. Montreal! Montreal was certainly the ideal locale for a party. During the last medical conference in Montreal they had had such a good time none could remember anything specific. Everyone just woke up back at home with receipts for expensive music and dance shows in their pockets.

Thanks for visiting, read the note of one particularly forgetful scientist, *your undergarments will be washed, pressed, and returned by tomorrow evening, signed Lilylivered Lori {(who cries at each story) but never the ones that are frightful or gory}.* Sure enough, the scientist's garments arrived at his door a moment after the stroke of midnight. Never before had his underpants made him feel so much like Cinderella.

"Food?"

"Xanax Zucchini and Asp-burgers and cheese!"

"Prozac Punch and Potato Autisticks!"

"Lithium Lasagna and Hallucinogenic Halvah!"

After a short melee, the Scientists finally agreed on Tourette's Tacos with Valium Salsa but could not decide on entertainment. On one hand, Loretta's fourth embodiment, Steamboat Meg {(with a paddle for a leg) won't work as well with a whittled tentpeg}, was partial to 80's progressive funk and Japanese acid jazz. On the other hand, it was well known that Loretta's sixth embodiment, Crankshaft Shelley {(with a bean in her belly) she bought a pet ringworm on her trip to New Delhi}, would not stay in a room unless 75% of the men were paying attention to her. The Scientists knew that she, among all of Loretta's personalities, was the most attractive by far, attractive enough to be an actress. Alas, she could only enjoy parties with stripper music and a designated stripper pole.

The party began by word of mouth. Whispering turned into susurration turned into discussion turned into yells. Fun broke out on the horizon like a toddler breaks from its mother's hands into the light of traffic. The Pierre Curie Postal Office was procured by the Scientists with funding provided by the Montreal Office of Fun Fun Funaround. Prostitutes were hired to douche and don waitress jackets. Disarranged old men, otherwise prone to troublesome idling, were encouraged to hang about outside the post office door wearing monocles and expensive stopwatch knock-offs to wrinkle their noses at passing ne'er-do-wells.

At exactly midnight, doll-faced drummers dressed as gypsies arrived fashionably early. Traintrack Tony {(who's jelly and bony) rides on the bus with an Alsatian buck-pony} brought his entire collection of white-noise 8-tracks unasked. The Scientists sent him in a van across the United States border to get private health care pharmaceuticals and Milwaukee beer. The drummers mingled and danced like maniacs, danced like freaks. A single floating soul moved from the dance floor to the punch bowl, back and forth and forth, wondering aloud at the cheap lighting, a fragmented disco ball.

Bellbottomed Bill {(lives in the whiskey still) licks the floor for a dizzying thrill} set up shop in the corner preparing breakfast endlessly. Morning, noon and night he toiled: pancakes, pancakes and more pancakes. Bill used them fungibly, like cash, to purchase gasoline, candles and other basic necessities. He could sell eight pancakes for the ingredients towards the next pancake batch which might provide sixteen large tasty pancakes. This pancake system promised to multiply and reproduce. Bill thought happily: I will never eat breakfast alone. In the bathroom of the Pierre Curic Postal Office, he opened a restaurant called Pavlov's Padlock and served breakfast for free save for eight pancakes he shoved into the cash register every morning earmarked for tomorrow's groceries. He told his son, Knockneed Ned {(who seduces the dead) repeats with scorn what's just been said}: one always replenishes stocks, that's just good business.

In the real world, meaning, when the party slowed and then flipped, Bill invited Loretta to a pancake party. "But only half of you," he insisted, "There are just too many mouths to feed otherwise." Loretta shook her head in confusion. She couldn't order the other personalities around, some had quite independent notions. But at least two of them were too snobby for words, and refused to be caught in the same general mindframe. One of them, Bug-eyed Sharon {(who can't stop starin') if she spots a canary she'll probly go barren} would not go to sleep without full makeup applied. Mushmouth Mark {(with a snout like a shark) he jabbers like a turkey on a shelf in the dark} would not live in a house without a toilet cast from 24-karat solid gold.

Diane and Dennis came as a lark. They were mostly normal, which is to say one personality per brain, one brain per body. They each pretended to be single at the party. It was Diane's idea.

"Later we'll laugh our asses off," she said to Dennis that afternoon when he crawled out of bed. He didn't tell her that, at the moment, he felt suicidal. He knew she didn't want to hear it. Life is nothing, he reasonably felt like explaining, just the pushing off of a nervous breakdown.

"Will you laugh at me?" he asked. She was trying on shiny negligees, black and red, in her pocket mirror.

"You mean now, with that pathetic hound-dog frown?"

Dennis felt sick. He was always asking questions he knew the answer to. "At the party."

"Of course. You're pathetic, aren't you?"

Diane was the meanest woman Dennis knew.

Later, they drove over fashionably late. There was a small problem at the door when they arrived, but Diane bared her teeth at the doorman and explained, "If you couldn't tell, I'm Satan's sister." The doorman stepped aside and allowed ingress.

Skirting the dance floor, Dennis approached the drinks table where two bowls sat, one with punch and ladle, and one with electrolytic jelly and a swimming brain which was stimulated and massaged by a battery that would never die. The punch bowl manned the brainjelly bowl, one drink per person. Dennis enjoyed the free booze, but mostly he regretted associating himself with Diane. He knew she would make a grown man cry by the end of the night; she kept a tally in a little spiral notebook. Now Diane started dancing with four men at once. She played them off each other like hypnotized puppy dogs. Dennis watched from the side drinking his brainjelly. In the blue tracklighting everything looked pale, even dead. The shadows in the room started to tilt and then it became an engaging experience. Fatass Philip {(who can't do a situp) eats a popcorn tub and can't even get up} danced over to Diane and asked if she wanted a drink. Dennis cringed because he knew Philip was dead meat. Diane laughed in his blubbery face and Philip ran away to cry.

At Pavlov's, Philip crammed a pancake into his mouth and complained, "How come everybody's having sex but me?" It made Dennis feel terrible how much enjoyment he knew Diane would get from hearing that comment. Bellbottomed Bill offered little consolation: "It's better to be attractive."

Diane saw Dennis's sympathetic face and she gave him a philosophical look which suggested: *weak people choose weakness and are not to be pitied*. She laughed cattily and all the men became nervous and horny. Dennis relented: "Her cruelty is gorgeous. How wonderful to be free from the spiritual world!" He never understood why she picked him, of all people, to terrorize in private life.

Crankshaft Shelley arrived and was instantly displeased by the attention Diane garnered. "It isn't fair," she complained to the Scientist ushers, "she's obviously psychotic! It's the easy way out."

Diane leaped onto the stage. "I'm married!" she screamed into the microphone, "Losers!"

With this information loosed, the party took an instant left turn.

Watching her strut on the stage in her negligee Dennis thought, *Maybe she doesn't get out enough.* When Diane laughed with her mouth wide, it reminded him of a yawning crocodile with big flappy lips; less beautiful, more like exotic and perilously thrilling. He thought he should make a sign for her neck: *Will work for insults.*

Diane screamed, "My job here is to induce sanity!"

God! Dennis thought, *she's making me sick.* He suddenly decided he wanted a divorce. Her normal-person craziness was way crazier than any insane-person's craziness. *Their* unpredictabilities were, at least, in a way, predictable. Plus the nymphomaniac chicks at the party seemed really wild. Crankshaft Shelley did a headstand belly-dance and licked Dennis' torso. Globetrotting Lydia {(with army-issued chlamydia) she invites you home only to get rid'a'ya} had contortioned herself into a pretzel and hummed alluringly in the pretzel bowl. Oldmaid Maria {(with insurmountable diarrhea) she eats only cherries on flour tortilla} asked Dennis if she could stick her arm into his mouth all the way to the elbow. He declined but with hesitation and a real sense of intrigue. She apologized seductively and brought him a fresh brainjelly drink. Newly desired, Dennis felt like a little boy with a chocolate coin in his heart. Clink goes the chocolate coin.

Diane walked over. Her eyes glittered. "What's going on?" She didn't like Dennis having adventures while she was on the stage, all that licking and seductive apologetics and nymphomaniacal inclinations. Plus, Dennis' pants were at half mast. She grabbed his pants' waist and Slaphappy Sam {(with a head like a ham) his nose like a boat but he don't give a damn} helped hoist them.

"Forget it, Diane, it's over. This is a real woman! She loves me for my sexy body and not because I'll pick her up groceries on my way home from work. That's love! I have to practically beg you just to gobble like a chicken."

"Turkeys gobble, chickens buck-buck. Anyway, that's not a real woman. That's a row of coats on a coatrack. I think you've had one too many Brainjelly Punch Bombs."

Diane took the drink away and helped him lift his pants. "When we get married and have a kid, we'll call her Auntie Depressant. What do you think?"

"Won't people think she's our aunt?"

"Maybe, but don't you think it's funny?"

"Not really. But if you say so, dear."

Later, after Dennis had passed out, Diane shared a table at Pavlov's with Hillbilly Ben {(and his flute-playing hen) don't let its sex parts too near old men}. She told him about her favorite gag: "So I cut apples into little heads. After they dry up all wrinkled, I stick these rag bodies on them and douse them in ketchup. Then I hang them over Dennis's bed. They look like bleeding witches and sometimes he'll shit himself in the morning if it works right. Can you believe it, it's not even Halloween! Aren't I funny? But now I'm thinking that maybe I won't attach bodies next time. Bodiless has charm too, don't you think?" Hillbilly Ben nodded and helped Diane carry Dennis to the car.

The couple began their way home. The night was as rich and dark as chocolate. The roads were like a benevolent schematic, a child's game with candy rewards. As the car pulled out of the parking lot, the gypsy drummers broke from the party and bifurcated. They yodeled at the blinking lights overhead: "Stars or Planes!"

It promised to be a long ride home. Diane saw in her husband's swoon exhaustion beyond the routine navigations. She drove with her hand on his knee. She was mortally frightened that Dennis would disappear into the night's manic jazz, those clefts and notes soldiering two-by-two. He was the anchor to her cruelty and she could not afford to lose him. She opened his head and massaged his brain with an electrolytic finger. "Clink goes the chocolate coin," she said hopefully and Dennis blinked his half-opened eye, a not-untender acquiescence.

Thank You Doctor Shockley

Dear Dr. Shockley,

Thank you for treating my monkey bites. I was afraid that I had tetanus or rabies or the jumping disease. Just know: if you get one monkey upset, sometimes a whole treeful will get upset, too. And they know the human weak points. Think of it this way: if you're covered with a hundred angry monkeys, that's eight hundred little fingers. People think monkeys are unintelligent but that's not true. They know how to undo belts and buttons and zippers. Thank God I passed out. But it was my fault. Contrary to popular television knowledge, most monkeys do not want to be elaborately-dressed house-servants. They are not as good-natured as some people think. They ate my maps and all my pixie-sticks.

As a thank-you present, I am sending you a *Buddha on the Toilet* that I bought in Little Thailand (in Birmingham, Alabama). I could have probably bought the same thing in Thailand for a tenth of the price, and also probably from one of the shops around the corner from your clinic, and saved myself a bunch on postage, but I didn't want you to think I was skimping on a gift. This *Buddha on the Toilet* is made of higher quality plastic than they have available in Thailand. I think the poor quality of Thailand plastic-products is shameful. Is the Buddha in the *Buddha on the Toilet* straining? Does his face show satisfied contemplation? Like the Mona Lisa, the toilet habits of the Buddha are an utter mystery.

I never finished telling you the story of how I got to Thailand and came to be taunting treemonkeys. Six months ago, when I heard about my great-aunt Theodora's revelation, I was working at this Persian-owned factory in New York City making progressive mannequins—three-legged mannequins, dwarf mannequins, eyeless, some with their tits cut off, or covered with fur, or with both penis and vagina. We were three weeks away from going public on the New York Stock Exchange. A lot of Germans were into our art. We were discussing terms with the Dutch Canoe Co. It was exciting stuff. I left the company at that time because they were branching into religious sex dolls: Jesus, Buddha, Mohammed, Moses, all the big ones. I just wasn't comfortable.

Then, suddenly, I caught word that Aunt Theodora was the next incarnation of the Dalai Lama. Nobody even called me. I learned it from her answering machine out-going message. Can you believe the humility? If I was the brand-new Dalai Lama I'd shout it from the rooftops. But not my Aunt Theodora. She probably wouldn't have even advertised it on the answering machine except that she was afraid people who needed healing would wonder where she was.

Well, it turned out she was in Tibet. "What a trip!" I said to myself, "I have to see this for myself." It was the first time an old white lady got the call. Generally, Dalai Lamas are male and Tibetan. Aunt Theodora would be the last person I would guess, because she basically spends her days drinking Martinis and playing mahjongg. Sometimes she'll invite her friends over to watch a DVD of General Hospital but I've never really known her to have a spiritual side other than visiting Carrie, her palm reader. Maybe there was some mystical spirituality in the mahjongg? But I feel really close to Aunt Theodora, always did. She used to let me and my friends see her naked. When she was younger and also after. That was really cool of her and I made a lot of friends in Middle and High School from that arrangement. She always had a free spirit, a Dalai Lama-like free spirit.

What happened was her husband, Uncle Mason, who used to be a short-order cook but is losing his sense of culinary art these days, believe me, had bought a package of toilet cookies which he served with her tea one morning. He said he thought they were frosted scones and I honestly believe there was no ill-intent. But it is difficult to reconcile Uncle Mason going to Home Depot for a package of frosted scones. I'm no French chef, and in fact, I usually can't wait for the microwave to *beep* and the food to cool off before I shove it in my mouth, but I know Home Depot doesn't carry scones, frosted or otherwise.

Dr. Shockley, are you familiar with toilet cookies? Well, I'll tell you, they're basically the single most chemically concentrated object on this planet, especially the blue ones. I'm told by a nuclear scientist friend that they could stand in for high-grade plutonium if need be. They also happen to be A-plus hallucinogen on par with peyote distilled in cough syrup, Magic Marker smell, and air conditioning refrigerant. When my Aunt Theodora ate that toilet cookie she had some religious reawakening. She stayed naked for a week before heading to Tibet to get her religious groove on.

When I heard that Aunt Theodora got the calling, I jumped on a midnight flight to Thailand. It turns out that Thailand is not even close to Tibet but I was too excited to check a map. I've been wanting to buy my own bike shop for three years now, so I can finally get in shape. I figured the Dalai Lama was someone who could definitely help that dream come true, through spiritual or political means, whichever.

Well, it turns out that Thailand is basically a really small country where everyone feels spiritual about not using modern toilets. I'm sure you know, Dr. Shockley. It wasn't easy finding my way around. Those people communicate, like, through rice, or something.

The most interesting part was that on my third day there, I met this yogi who was into molesting tourist girls. It turned out this guy used to work in the same mannequin factory as me. Isn't that a wild coincidence? While I was there he gave me the grand tour. See, he taught these Western girls how to get lost in transcendence in one-on-one lessons, with the slow breathing and the mind-numbing mantras so that they got into this half-gone state of mind, man, pretty much disappearing from the material world, and then he'd feel them up and give them gel-baths or shave their legs with Crisco. He was a real sick fuck if you want to know the truth.

They caught him eventually by following the trail of Crisco. This guy could burn through a case in a week. And he wasn't recycling, the asshole, so they found over 600 empty tubs of the stuff buried in his backyard.

Dr. Shockley, anyway the ending is kind of sad. It turned out that Aunt Theodora is not the Dalai Lama, it was false alarm, so I guess no bike shop for me. I have to think of another way to get in shape once this thing blows over. My backup plan was to ship treemonkeys back to America for sale to blind people or circuses, but anyway, you know how that turned out.

These days I've been carting bags of dirt into Uncle Mason's and Aunt Theodora's house to scatter around. It's too clean! Every time my Aunt Theodora vomits the place smells like it's been run through a carwash.

>Thanks again,
>Bill Watkins,
>The Guy with Forty-four
>Monkey Bites
>(face, stomach and buttocks)

Jimmy Dreams

Former President Jimmy Carter wakes in night. The clock on the table reads 12:38. He sits in the dark for a moment, the utter silence, and then closes his eyes. He knows a willing of sleep is futile. He rolls over and bumps his wife gently. She turns with a start.

"Wha? S'you OK?"

"Yeah." He is too proud to tell his anxieties. He knows, after all these years of marriage, she will sense his troubled mind. She takes a moment to clear her head and then sits up, places the pillow behind her back.

"You need your sleep dear. You have a long flight tomorrow."

"I know."

"What's wrong?" It has been months since he and Rosalyn have talked. He cannot confess that he cannot express his need, that his need needs teasing out.

"Not anything, really."

"I heard the trip to Guatemala went well. I heard they roasted a pig in your honor."

"Yes. They were very hospitable."

"I should think so. You helped build their hospital."

"Yes. They were very nice people, very warm." Jimmy speaks quietly and tonelessly.

Rosalyn squeezes his hand. "Do you want me to make you a cup of tea?"

"No thank you." He reaches for a book of short stories on the bedside table that he has been reading. The book is called *Return* by Kenny Kissens. All the stories in the book have a ghost that returns from the netherworld to haunt characters in this world.

"I want to tell you about this story. It's been bothering me."

Jimmy and Rosalyn once owned a ritual to read out loud in bed, though never this late at night.

"It's a very strange story."

His wife scoots downward on the bed so she is prone again. "I'm closing my eyes but I'm listening."

He opens the book at the bookmark and skims the text, remembering the taste of the story. "The story is too long to read the whole thing. I'm not even sure if it's any good or worthwhile. It's so bizarre."

"Mm-hmm."

"It begins with Mark Twain on his deathbed."

"Mark Twain?"

"Yes, *the* Mark Twain. He's lying in bed, preparing to die, and his wife, Olivia, is tending to him. She presses a wet towel to his forehead and he has this look…" Jimmy hesitates and shifts his body.

She responds with closed eyes, "Uh-huh. Mark Twain. He's dying. I'm listening…"

"…and he has this appearance, you know, on his face, that before he dies he wants to say something significant, something definitive, to his wife…"

Jimmy jostles his wife gently. She appraises him with a motherly eye. "Yes… something significant." She closes her eye.

"Olivia recognizes this and leans in close to his lips. He says, 'If I have one wish, it is that one person reads one of my stories one day after I die. That is all I ask.' You see, because he wanted to leave a legacy in his writing."

"Um-hmm."

"Then he dies. And this is when the story gets bizarre. His wife is surprisingly affected by his death, and she collects all of his books from all over the world and destroys them. She does not want his wish to come true; she does not want to share him. Then, Mark Twain's ghost…"

Rosalyn chortles and Jimmy glances at the front cover of the book: *Return* by Kenny Kissens.

"…the ghost comes back the next day. He's very upset at what his wife has done, though, as a ghost, he cannot tell her. He then visits his hometown to see if any of his books remain, if perhaps there is a man or woman who, because of sentimentality, would not allow Olivia to destroy his book. The ghost spends a full day poking around and when he is about to give up he sees a grown man, a retarded man, flipping through his stories on the banks of the river. Somehow, this man-child has gotten his hands on the last Mark Twain book."

Jimmy scratches his eyebrow, "Really, it's without explanation." He clucks disapprovingly. "…Anyway, this halfwit reads the story and then throws his copy of *Tom Sawyer* into the Mississippi river. Done. That is the last remaining copy of Mark Twain's writing. But the ghost is not sad, quite the opposite, he is happy, because he stuck to his dying words: 'If I have one wish it is that at least one person reads one of my stories one day after I die.'

"I'm a little confused at what comfort the eyes of a retarded man could bring Mark Twain. But he is a man of integrity and he won't quibble about parting wishes… His legacy lived on, after all. Do you see?"

Rosalyn does not answer.

"…He broke the confines of death, in a way. He made his

own rules."

Jimmy sits in the darkness.

"…But then, of course, the story gets even more bizarre…" Jimmy listens to the echo of his voice in the bedroom. The lack of response to his words in the night air strikes him with great force. He thinks suddenly of all the nights spent awake, all the nights spent waiting for the dark to answer.

"…Mark Twain has seen his dying wish come true but he does not return to the netherworld. The Powers That Be, apparently, have something else in mind. So he wanders the Earth for another generation. His wife, Olivia, meanwhile, becomes a publishing baroness and she passes this company on to her children, who further pass it on, until it's the present day and the Twain family is the owner of the largest publishing company in the world. Billionaires…" Jimmy nods and flips through the novel's pages.

"…Very bizarre, you see, like science fiction, because Samuel Clemens was an inventor, after all. In publishing… Are you up, dear?"

His wife does not answer.

"But it descends after that. The plot gets rather juvenile…"

He puts the book on the bedside table, "Well, anyway, this ghost of Mark Twain, who has been walking the Earth for close to a century without knowing why, suddenly gets it into his head that he's supposed to change the publishing industry. That this billion dollar company owned by his family is soulless and without integrity. No good writing could come from them. You see, they publish the trashy books you see in the supermarket aisles, the romances and cheap mysteries with the glossy pictures. Soap opera drivel. The ghost of Mark Twain begins haunting these trashy writers and then the book gets violent." Jimmy reaches for the book and reads the back cover:

Return is Kenny Kissens' second book. Much praise has

been given this young author for his first book *The Candyland Glorifications*. Kenny lives in London with his first wife, Amelia, and their daughter, Olivia.

Jimmy continues, "I don't like these violent parts. These young writers are deliberately shocking, it seems...

"...The ghost travels around the globe murdering all of these trashy writers who work for his family's publishing business. He begins with an author of courtroom dramas—causes a bus to run him over..."

Jimmy looks to his wife. Her chest rises and falls with regular breathing. "...Then he drowns this married couple who write shoddy mysteries. Afterwards, he hangs a romance writer and each of the assistants who help her regurgitate a fresh novel every month. And then it ends there. Mark Twain's ghost is allowed to return to Heaven, or wherever he was earlier... Limbo, perhaps... It's bloody and a bit upsetting. I'm not entirely glad I read it.

"It had its interesting moments, though. Mark Twain's comments about integrity, his revulsion to works of poor quality. Twain was a special man; a man of principle; a rarity of character."

Jimmy slides down the bed so that he is in a sleeping position.

"...So I suppose the book has some redeeming quality."

Having concluded the story, Former President Jimmy Carter stares at the ceiling, at its shadowy colorlessness. Even with his wife by his side, he feels hopelessly lonely. He knows that he will get up tomorrow and board the plane to Uruguay. He will be on time and he will probably feel better. There is a voice in his head that tells him to go to sleep. *The terrible feeling will fade. Why dwell on bad thoughts? It is not practical. There is work to be done and you need your rest.* But tonight he is stubborn. There is so much pragmatism in his life already, too much. It is clear he is not like the character of Mark Twain. He has no force of tongue, no wit, no righteous anger. Never much of a poetry reader, he thinks of the line by T.S. Eliot, *Should I have the strength to force the moment to its crisis?* Like Prufrock he could never force the issue. He is only an everyday sort of worker, a grunt. But what crisis? he thinks, And where does one begin?

He remembers a young Indian man he met in Calcutta who offered a discussion of literature.

"I like the German leader Hitler's writing," the Indian man said, "What is it called? *Mein Kampf*."

"Why?" He was flabbergasted. "The man was crazy."

"Yes," The Indian man nodded, unashamed and unknowing, "but he had such power in his speech."

Jimmy turns away from his wife and thinks sadly: Even craziness can be discounted, even evil. The only thing remembered is hate, the power of hate. How sad. He brings the bedcover to his neck, hides his face beneath. I will never be one of those who blaze with passion, who start wars with well-timed and charismatic phrases. I am no revolutionary, no fist-pounder in the courtroom. I could never distill life of its juice, like squeezing an orange. I won't be one of those men, who, when they die, cause the planet's spin to skip a beat, who disrupt the very rotation of the Earth.

Jimmy urges himself towards purposelessness, towards some conclusive realization, towards an overwhelming.

"Nothing matters," he thinks with courage and fear, "it's all a terrible joke."

The feeling is too much. In terror, he holds himself motionless in bed. He is trembling. His chest aches and he cries out.

"Wha? Whas wrong?"

Instantly, Rosalyn's cotton-mouth soothes him. She is confused like him. He feels centered once again in this world, vital once more. There is no escaping moments of weakness; in the gray, anonymous night we all are vulnerable like homeless children.

"Nothing," he says, "I am fine. Let's go back to sleep."

Listening To My Son

I have his license. I know I'm going to lose it. I'll make a photocopy. I can hear him now in his room. He's lying in his cot just like I'm lying in my cot. He's on his side, with his elbows underneath his head, staring at the wall. The wall helps him go empty, keep a distance from the empty. He doesn't think about life like me. He works on that not thinking. When he gets older it'll come over him slowly, whether he's in prison or not, the thinking about life. It'll come over him slowly, how his body gets weaker, like all our bodies get weaker, and then he'll have that sad knowledge about life.

I can lay my cheek against the cool concrete walls. Any time I want I can place him, which room he's in, listening to the whispers of the drafty hallways. If he's eating dinner or lifting weights. If he's smoking marijuana. The air tells me because I'm his father. I can lay my cheek to the concrete wall with the peeling lemon paint. I can follow him in the prison with my knowledge. I stay true to his mother by watching. She visits him every week and me once a month. When she cries without tears she can see into my face, how my face is solid like a guard, because I've been listening in the long concrete hallways, the steps up and down all the rooms, listening to the sighs of my son. She knows I do my duty to the listening. I'm forgiven for leaving him behind.

I need to make a photocopy of his license before I lose it. Every night I lie in my cot and wonder of he'll die in an ugly way. I want to have that photocopy with me when he dies. I have bad luck with important things, they all seem to get lost.

That's the thing I don't want for my son. To die in an ugly way, with a razor or a nail, some dirty crazy man standing over him giving a dead-eye look, if he takes the life from my son in one fell swoop. One of those guys with a blade, eyeballs bugging from juice, greasy hair, skinny arms scraggled with tattoos, thinking he's the messenger of the Lord, a prince of darkness. I want to take my son by the shoulders in the yard during break and shake him: "Watch out for those stupid men with knives. Don't get killed in an ugly way!" But if I touch him on the shoulder, he gives me a bitter face because he hates me. He doesn't know that I listen to him through the air, to his steps in his cell, back-and-forth, like he could forget his troubles. I hear all his sad hopeless breaths and I know he can't hate his father. He doesn't understand about the listening yet. When he's older his mother will say so. She'll say so without saying.

If he gets killed in prison I can't help him. I don't have the strength like I used to. I'm older now, an old man, and life already stole my life. I couldn't stand under a beating. I couldn't give a beating. I'm just waiting it out, listening to the angry strength of my son, among all these angry men, how his anger gets quieter each day, draining into the air. I listen to the air in the concrete hallways, I hear how angry he gets because he sees it grow weaker, how the angriness leaves by seconds, how it's my fault because he was born to a weak father. Once I was a bear of a man, I had the teeth and muscles of a king bear. Now I'm a listener. My son thinks listening is a sign of weakness.

Every night I lie in my cot and stare at the ceiling and wonder if my son will die in an ugly way. I get scared to God. I get so scared and I call out to God, "Don't let my son die like a rat!" My son has an angry face, even when he talks to me, or at the phone with his mother. I know he's asking to die in an ugly way. I'm too scared to think about it. Sometimes when I'm sick with a cough and I'm feeling weak, I'll think: "Is that *my* same angry face? Did I give him that?" People used to say that about me, about how I couldn't be reasoned with, about how I was locked inside, how the bear was there, wild like a mountain king, a mangy mountain king, the anger turning crazy because its not meant to be in a cage. It's meant to be free, King of all Free, that's what I was. Now is different, now I see it again, my son like a caged animal, starting to know in the way of older people, how the anger is robbed from us, in front of our eyes, leaving life by the second. We've got no say in the matter. I see how things come back on the owner. The sins of the parents return on the children. There's a deeper justice at play here, behind the scenes, bigger than judges and lawyers, but I can't tell him those things. It only comes through listening to the air, listening for the movements of the ones you love, losing life by the second.

My son's face looks like he ate something bitter, a bitter poison, which is slowly killing. I don't tell him what I know, try to calm him down. I understand how he has to hate all the world. What choice is there? You can't blame the lawyers or the guards or the judge. You have to blame someone. God has to know, or someone has to know, that it's not fair to make a man witness his life leave by seconds. To make a man a king bear, only to rob him slowly. I see how it is to be young, and I'm glad I'm not asked to do it all again. That's for the young to do, try to keep life alive with blame and hate. It's too plain for an old man like me.

    I don't blame the prison or guards or the judge. Life steals life. You can't hide in here, that's the bare downside. It's a plain kind of knowing. The peeling lemon paint for the concrete walls. The drafty hallways with the air always the same, hovering between happening and not happening; full of frozen, useless violence. You have to watch, you're forced to listen. That's really what the judge said for my assault and battery, and for my son's armed robbery. "You are hereby sentenced to watch your life leave by seconds."

Dara Come Home

Dara, I'm sorry that I screamed in the movie theater. The man wouldn't close the exit doors and the movie was already playing. That religious hush makes me insane. I hear names in the semi-dark. It's too much anticipation.

Dara, I'm sorry I yelled. I know it was my fault. But I just want to tell you the story of the movie. Afterwards it felt like it matched up with my yelling, my reason for yelling. It's a coincidence I have to share.

The movie was about a sad girl. She looked kind of like you, with yellow hair and a down-turned mouth. She could never forget about her sadness, not even for a second, not even while looking at flower boutiques or boy-and-girl squirrels chasing each other through lawn sprinklers and up trees. She sat down one day to write a letter to her ex-boyfriend who had gone off to law school. Even though he promised not to, he had forgotten about her when he left. That was the day she suddenly realized that she was forgettable. It wasn't about love, you see, just about staying significant to a lover, leaving a mark behind, some nostalgia. But this guy couldn't wait to forget the sad girl. So she wrote this note to him about how she would never forget him, even though he had forgotten her. Even if he got a face-lift and traveled to another country, she would never forget him, how he would always be a good person in her eyes. She tried to explain her thoughts and feelings to this guy, how she can never forget painful things even though it's bad for her. Like, once, one of her students at school called her a *bitch*. Once her father screamed at her for hugging him at the wrong time. Her grandmother said something suggestive about her weight. Once her friend ignored her phone call. Many men, too many to count, disregarded her at lonely times. It wasn't that she held grudges; she just couldn't forget anything. She wrote in the letter how she was jealous of her ex-boyfriend that he could forget so easily, like the easy way he had forgotten her. *Lucky* is what she called it.

In the movie, this blind mailman was working at the post office. He knew all the post boxes by heart and could sort the mail faster than anyone else, by touch alone. He was also very charming. He made at least one joke to every customer. When it was the sad girl's turn in line, he told her that she smelled pretty. She blushed and sniffed her hand. When he heard that, he smiled. She bought a stamp and when she passed him the letter their hands touched. He coughed and told her how her skin made him think about Christ's hands, how they were soft and cool, not human but not unhuman. He said this in the post office with about six people waiting in line. She started crying. Then, after this blind postman got off work, she went home with him.

They started dating and having sex all the time. At first, it was just a prank sort of thing, like, how would it feel to have sex with a blind guy? But then it turned out that he was pretty good-looking with his shirt off, not that he cared or knew, and his eyes were a scary sort of black, like puddles of india ink. Sometimes when she looked at him, if he was up in the middle of the night, sitting on the bed, halfway in the moonlight, near the meaningless window, he looked like he had no feelings, that the world made him feel dead. She cried for him a lot, about how unjust God was, because he would never see hot-air balloons lifting off or fish breathing underwater. But he told her, "Don't feel bad for me. I'm happy to be with you. I don't feel bad for myself, so why should you?"

I forgot to tell you that this lonely girl wasn't really much to look at. That was one of the reasons her old boyfriend left. He went to law school so he could get rich and marry a beautiful woman that he could show off at law firm parties. This lonely girl was a little fat and the blind guy said he kind of liked that. He didn't know better. He had never even seen a supermodel in his whole life! After a week, he told her he liked the way her pussy smelled. Can you believe a blind guy would say that?

But the main thing was that this lonely girl liked to imagine what the blind guy saw during sex, how his orgasms looked. Did he see colors during sex, like shooting stars, or black-ribboned rainbows, or electrical sparks, or nothing, like a different kind of nothing than the regular nothing? It doesn't make sense to me, because *no one* really sees anything during orgasm, like fireworks exploding or impressionist paintings or visions of ancient Greece. At least I never did. But thinking about that kind of thing got her off.

Then, she started wearing all these crazy clothes. He taught her not to care what people think, like her family or people on the street, like if they frowned when they saw her wearing old or mismatched clothes. Except when he was wearing his postman uniform, the blind guy had a knack for clashing on purpose. Horizontal stripes with vertical stripes, different shades of white. He didn't care. He only wore clothes that made him feel good. He loved these gold boots and he was big into headbands.

In the end of the movie he got run over by a mail truck. His best friend ran him over. But the lonely girl felt OK about the world because she had met such an amazing man. I kind of didn't get that part. It was a stupid ending. It made me think about if *you* got run over by a mailtruck, how would I feel... But I already know. I'd feel that the world was dead.

Dara, I should have followed you when you ran out of the theater. I don't even know why I stayed for such a shitty movie. I must be crazy or fucked-up or something. I'll never forget you, Dara, even if you don't get this letter.

Soldier Jerry
and His Steed Bessie Ann

Jerry worked in an office pushing papers back and forth, organizing, copying, faxing. It was a fairly unclassy job that any semi-intelligent person could do. The other guy who did the same job was known as having an IQ below 70: a retarded man. But mostly Jerry didn't care. Sometimes he'd sign for a package from the FedEx guy and feel pretty important. Conversely, sometimes he'd have to mop up a bathroom stall and feel kinda low. So mostly he was glad with the paperpushing and filing because there wasn't much to mess up.

Way back in high school, he used to have big dreams. When he was nineteen and studying car repair a few hours a day and getting loaded a whole lot and going to *Mac Karrie's* to sing karaoke on Wednesday nights, he met Doreen and she asked him what his dream was. "I'm gonna be like Elvis," he said and meant it. He thought his karaoke was getting pretty damned good. Doreen had laughed at him but he married her anyway because she let him have sex at a NASCAR tournament under a blanket. It was hot; they humped right near a whole crowd of people.

Jerry had a small pre-fab house on Miner Street that looked like every other house on the block. It was shaped in a cube, and let in all the summer's sun and all the winter's frost. Jerry lived with Doreen and their two girls, Kali and Jillian. Doreen worked part-time as a secretary for a lawyer. Nine years ago, at the office July Fourth picnic, Jerry won the softball game for his team with a mean double down the first base line, and the head boss patted him on the back. He had been *good* in high school in softball, but there's no professional league for men. In bed that night he turned to Doreen and cried, "I just love sports so much." That was the night Kali was conceived. Sports was the only topic that the real workers at work would let him talk about in the coffee corner.

Between the two paychecks, Jerry and Doreen could have afforded to move from Miner Street if they had planned well. Doreen's mother even offered to pay the moving costs. She said, "I'll pay so long as you get those children to a city block without drug dealers setting up shop on every corner." Doreen had never seen a drug dealer on their street but she was beginning to come around; they were one of the few white families in the neighborhood. Jillian was acting crazy, wearing sports bras out in public, and she was seeing at least three boys of different ethnicities. She was talking with a foreign-sounding accent at the breakfast table which Doreen's mother didn't like. Jerry didn't care. All of Jillian's boyfriend's were small guys he could easily beat up.

One day, to Jerry's surprise, the retarded guy in the office got promoted. Jerry knew the guy was related to a head boss but it still made him feel like shit. He felt like everybody but him, even retarded guys, moved up in the company. The quality control staff tried to teach Jerry the computer program that they bought to replace the old worker, but Jerry had no patience for computers, and every day he felt more and more useless.

One day, during the ride home in the Civic that Doreen's mother had bought, Jerry saw a billboard ad for the Hummer semi-military vehicle. It was a stupendous machine. The billboard showed its front-tire stirring up a cloud of dust as it just about busted through the sign. Jerry's heart went wild with desire. He felt like a teenager again and he and his friends were peeping on hot Holly Fitzer from his father's rooftop with Pete Keegan's half-broken telescope. Jerry drove immediately to the Hummer dealership, traded in his Civic for a couple hundred bucks, and drove away with a brand new Hummer. He felt powerful and manly when he drove, kind of like a warrior on a steed. Jerry's father had been in the Korean War, and Jerry had always felt that if he had stuck to discipline, he could have made a go in the army. But it didn't matter now. Bessie Ann was enough military vehicle for anyone. His new baby *transformed* him into a soldier. Driving Bessie Ann was like driving a small battleship. If he wanted to, he could run over those tiny Japanese cars, four at a time, like a monster truck. Whenever he got into Bessie Ann and fought for positioning on the highways, Jerry remembered: Life *is* war.

All during work, he'd dream about getting into Bessie Ann and driving around like a real man. In the car, he'd put on Lynyrd Skynyrd or Deep Purple, head out to the highway and really open her up. The gas was expensive but that was the Arabs' fault. That's why God made the wrath of war.

After a week, Jerry felt more at home in the Hummer than at his real home with his family. He felt that Bessie Ann was like a moving home. Once he let Jillian sit on his lap while he drove because she was his favorite next to Bessie Ann. But he didn't like Doreen or Kali even getting inside the car because they didn't know how to respect it.

When the United States went to war in Iraq, Jerry was especially glad to own Bessie Ann. It all made sense: a man's got to protect what's his. Jerry went out and bought himself a gun. He kept it in the glove compartment. The gun was black like Bessie Ann; a matching set. When he listened to the radio broadcast of the war on his way to work, he laid the gun within reach on the front seat. He began to think that he was in the war and that the Arabs had made it to the States.

Jerry stared down each pedestrian he passed. He knew which ones were bombers; it was the look on the face. He began to realize that assassins could just as easily find him at work. If he heard footsteps around the corner of the office hallway he would jump out and confront them: HIYA! Then the other workers started looking at him funny and he had to cool it. But he realized that most Americans don't even know the meaning of real danger.

Inside Bessie Ann he had the courage to realize how easy a threat could cripple his country. Behind each bush could be an Iraqi bomber. Behind each basement curtain could be a bomb factory. When an Arab cut him off in traffic one day he swerved to a stop and yanked the gun to the windshield. "Son of a bitch!" he yelled. He was milliseconds from blowing the fucking Iraqi's brains into sausage. The only thing that stopped him was two little kids in the Arab's backseat. It was a dirty move to bring his kids along but Jerry wouldn't kill him on principle. It was unpatriotic for kids to see a man's war.

When Jerry got home that day he was exhausted. He found he tolerated the presence of his wife and children so much more. Being hunted and smelling blood made him appreciate the simpler things in life.

Two weeks later, after being cut off in traffic, Jerry crashed the Hummer. There was an SUV coming towards him, driven by an Arab terrorist, so he swerved out of the way and hit a bus stop. The Hummer was totaled and he didn't have any insurance. He had to take a bus back home. He was sure that three men in the bus were thinking about strangling him. He felt for the gun hidden in his underwear. The cop didn't search him after the accident, just gave him the breathalyzer. At home, Jerry showed Doreen the gun. She didn't say anything for a full day but her fucking the next night got real excited. Jerry knew she liked the gun; she liked it even more than the Hummer. Jerry thought about taking the gun out during sex and sticking it at her belly, sticking it *in* her. He thought she'd probably cum her brains out.

A week later, Jerry began bringing the gun into work hidden in his underwear. He started talking about guns every day with the security guard. Only a man in a uniform could know, like Jerry, how serious the shit gets. And when the shit would come down and everybody would run for cover, they would have to back each other up. POW! POW! Jerry would take each of those bombers to the lobby floor; splatter their brains all over the office. And if the security guard got hit, even though he was a big fat guy, Jerry would carry him outside on his shoulders like a hero.

One day Jerry asked to see the security guard's gun. He brought out his own. They looked similar but Jerry's was half an inch longer. Jerry laughed and felt great. But the next day the head boss from upstairs came into Jerry's cubicle with two security guards and asked him to come upstairs for a personal meeting. The security guards were drinking coffee in front of the boss's office. They nodded to Jerry.

"He's gonna fire you and we're supposed to make sure you don't do anything crazy."

"Is it because of the gun?"

"You were jumping out of the bathroom and scaring people. You were jumping out of the elevator and the stairways. It's all on security tape. You were scaring everybody."

When Jerry walked towards the boss's office he felt like he was stoned, happy and excited beyond belief. He felt like he was making a true sacrifice for his beloved country and its purple fields of grain. He didn't even hear a word that came out of the boss's mouth. The security guards each took one of his elbows and escorted him downstairs, "Well, you gotta stay prepared for your country," he said, "You never know when you'll be called upon."

At the front door, free at last, he felt a melancholy sort of joy. He turned to the one security guard that was sort of his friend, "Brother, we gotta stay vigilant in times of war."

"Maybe so."

And they hadn't even taken away his gun.

For two months, Doreen got on Jerry's case about not having a job. He got mad enough one night to go looking for trouble. A black guy knocked into him at the 7-11 so he pushed him into an alley outside and shot him. The cops knocked on his door only two hours later. He was the only white man within four square blocks. They searched and found the gun. They brought him in to the station and it all matched up; an open and shut case.

He kept his head down for the first few months of prison. He didn't talk much. He had heard about homosexual rape.

After two years passed, a teenage girl named Bianca found his name on a website and wrote him a handful of letters. The letters drove him crazy; they were sexier than anything Doreen had ever done. Bianca came to visit him one morning. It wasn't a conjugal visit but she gave him a couple of photos. Jerry could tell it was a big deal for her to be inside the jailhouse; he could tell it made her horny as hell. She wrote a story about her love for Jerry for one of the teenage magazines, how it was so difficult and lonely for him in jail, and how his case was racially unfair. She sent him a copy. The picture they used was of Jerry at a softball game. Jerry was nineteen. In the photo, he held a bat and you couldn't help but notice his giant biceps. The magazine editors took out Doreen from the photo with a computer. Bianca explained that it was better for the teenage girls to think that he was single with no family. Jerry didn't mind. After they ran the article, he felt like a celebrity. He got over a hundred letters from teenage girls. Lots of them had sexy words if you knew how to read them right. When he talked to Doreen or his daughters on the phone he always mentioned his fans. He felt like Burt Reynolds or Elvis and he knew he would get laid like a king once he got out of jail.

The letters eventually stopped coming but Bianca still visited once. And even though her face was bony she had a pretty hot body.

Jerry thought of Bianca every night until he got out two years later. He tried to find her but she had left town. So had his wife. Jillian sent him forty bucks by Western Union and that made him feel pretty good for awhile because he was able to get back on his feet bagging groceries. He was glad he had let her sit in the Hummer twelve years ago because she remembered how he had always loved her, how she had always been his second favorite.

The Elderly Crisis

What has happened to this generation of old people?

There was a time when you could count on the elderly. Sure, they were a dirty bunch, full of complaints, patched together with Ace bandages, sour-smelling salves and mechanical osteoporosis rigging. But they were weak and meek and knew to stay out of the way.

Once upon a time, you could knock an old person down on the sidewalk or jump in front of them in the grocery line. No one would protect them because they were quote-unquote on-their-way-out. One time when I was in a shoe store, I made some old lady smell my dirty sock just to make my girlfriend laugh. Another time, my girlfriend broke a table lamp over an old man's head just to make herself laugh. But that was how it was back then. It was a world of youth and vigor, and a touch of snottiness could get you a seat to the Queen's buffet. Likewise, if an old person died in front of you, you didn't call an ambulance or a morgue, you just pushed their body to the gutter or the edge of the sidewalk. A group of people maybe stood around for a second and shrugged a lot.

Someone would say: "Oh, well, old people die. At least there's one less lonely person smelling up some lonely apartment," and then everyone'd do lines of cocaine. It was the 80's… no one cared so long as you turned the gnarled suffering face of the dead away from human traffic.

But something troubling has happened. Truly. Everywhere I turn it seems some old person is shoving me around or kicking me in the ass. Somewhere down the road old people got nasty. What year was it exactly? I couldn't tell you, though I have a feeling it has to do with that psychotic time warp created by *Matlock* having sex with *Murder She Wrote*. But it doesn't matter. Simply put: no more apple pie from grandma with the smell of mothballs and Ben-Gay baked into the crust. Sean Connery and Clint Eastwood run this show. If you ain't at least seventy you've got no business showing your face around the Playboy mansion. Mighty Hugh Hefner is dating lesbian sextuplets genetically fused at the nipples. And Old Charlie Heston drives around Malibu in a Commando tank.

Probably, it's the money that started it off. Old people are rich mainly because they were smart enough to collect rare coins back in the 20's: stacks of three-legged buffalo nickels, cowlick Roosevelt dimes, and cross-eyed Lincoln pennies, and they just sat on those coins till they turned into millions. Also many of them bought Microsoft Inc. and Ford Motor Co. stock back when they were called Rockefeller Electronic Thinking Machine and Superfast Bike Company and were dirt cheap. Some of them got in on polio vaccines and penicillin when they were brand new.

Now since they're super rich, old people can act as pushy and superior as they want. Old men pop penis-engorging drugs as fast as tic-tacs. They shoot up anabolic steroids in the gym club locker room where I belong and do uneven bar routines and gymnastic-horse dismounts.

Old women have the cash to buy expensive herbal supplements which induce prolonged spontaneous orgasms. Sometimes I'll see an old lady thrashing around on the K-Mart jewelry department floor and I'll think: *Man, I wish I was an old lady.*

Needless to say, both genders of old people are itchy with brand new never-before-seen-by-modern-science STDs: Wrinklimpy, Flassilia, Elderlyphilis. These STDs hide in the old people's wrinkly folds like cockleburs under a burro's saddle. It makes 'em irritable and out-of-control. Dear god, bring back the geezers and make right this upside-down world!

I don't even want to imagine it, but soon all the young beautiful girls in the world will be snatched up by gigantically muscular, exceedingly sexy old men. And all the young men will be chained at the neck by wealthy sex-starved sugar-mommas. I only hope, by the time that happens, that I'm an old man myself. I'm saving up my coins; I've got about thirty of each of those state-mascot quarters, except for Vermont and Puerto Rico. But in fifty years or so I imagine those coins will be worth millions. I sure hope so. Otherwise I'll probably end up chained at the neck by some hundred-and-fifty-year-old sex-starved sugar momma who looks like Jabba the Hut. If you want to know the truth I'm as tender as Princess Leia, maybe tenderer.

If I'm rich, it'll be OK. I'll sleep my way around the planet like the grizzled Grateful Dead. Then, when I'm really old and I've caught all the STDs, the fun can begin. Modern science has shown that when two 100-year-olds with STDs copulate, real magic takes place. There's a miraculous spark at the spot of their union, and they have a magic STD-baby made entirely of STDs. The heart, the eyes, the liver, all STDs. Then when the baby gets to be a teenager the elderly parents tell it to wear a condom when it has sex with other STD-kids so that it doesn't catch an STH, a sexually transmitted human.

Grandpa's Grandson

My grandfather always told me: "You can tell a lot about the character of a man by the consistency of his excrement." This was the best piece of advice I ever received. The second best was from my father: "Don't wear socks if the boots leak."

My grandfather was a janitor for the law firm *Crabtree, Deleuth and Delillian* for ten years. Before that he had worked in a health clinic in the Mojave Desert. I visited him once when I was thirteen, bar-mitzvah age, and there was a lot of talk about me turning into a man. Believe it or not, those Jewish people don't really tell you what being a *man* means which I think is something of a dirty trick. Sometimes I wish I had been in one of those African tribes where they just push you in to the forest when you hit thirteen and say, "If you live 'til tomorrow then you're a man." That way all you have to do is live for one night, maybe find a treelog to crawl into or a cave, and you've earned it. If you get mauled by a bear they probably even give you a decent *man*'s burial, not a kid's, y'know, because otherwise you might come back and haunt those fuckers who pushed you in… all in all, perfectly respectable.

But it's not so simple in the Jewish world. The only thing that's clear when you turn into a man is that you can't anymore look up girls' skirts. From my point of view there's nothing worth living for if you can't peek at girls' panties, which is why

I've never been much of a religious man.

Grandpa showed me around the Mojave Health and Serenity Clinic which was a retreat for rich people suffering from exhaustion. Old ladies who had never worked a day of their lives would show up, wave a wad of cash, and Grandpa would pack mud on their faces, give 'em steam showers and mineral baths, shave the body parts that were too hairy, pour hair tonic on the places that were not hairy enough, and generally oil them up so they feel like a newborn seal. A vacation at Mojave Health cost upwards of a nice car.

The next part of my grandpa's job was to poke through the rich people's doo-doo looking for what sort of minerals and vitamins might be missing from their diet. For instance, color tells you a lot. Green tint means low potassium while blue means low bilirubin. But his theory is that consistency is the most important and I'm not one to argue with the expert. As the old ladies left Mojave Health and Serenity Clinic he'd give them a printout of foods they should and should not eat. Like the report might say, *Eat walnuts and red vegetables but stay away from bananas and bread pudding.* Then an old woman might feel full of purpose in the grocery store as she steered clear of the bread pudding aisle and headed for the walnut section.

Grandpa got fired eventually for stealing some of Elvis's poop. "It was the best job I ever had," he said, "but the stakes were too high." In case you were wondering, Elvis was low on Niacin, but chock full of fiber. Elvis was the king of fiber. So anyway my grandpa came out east, did some interviewing, and Deleuth gave him a job cleaning the bathrooms at the law firm. Deleuth could tell right away he was an expert.

His son, my father, also worked scrubbing toilets at *Crabtree, Deleuth, and Delillian* for over twenty-eight years. Nowadays I work for them too in what might be called the family business. I've only been janitoring for two years but I'm learning from the best. Sometimes on federal holidays when nothing's good on TV and none of the parades have giant balloon animals that I care for, me and Grandpa will go down to the law firm so that he can teach me his know-how.

"You can't find this stuff in books or college, man, janitoring is either in your bones or it's not. Can't force what's not there. It'd be like flushing a tampon down a toilet... just ain't meant to be..."

Then we'll go to the executive washroom and poke around a bit and we compare those excrements to the excrements we find on the basement floor where all the lowlife criminals come in to have Crabtree, Deleuth or Delillian Esquires help them get out of paying child support or alimony. And what do you know, each time, you can tell the difference. Executive excrement is healthy and supple while criminal excrement is messy and troublesome. Each time, the character of the excrement is just like the character of the excretor. And I like to think that my excrement is solid and dependable because guess what: *I'm* solid and dependable.

When he was on his deathbed I asked my grandpa for some last words. He handed me his trusty scrubber as a heirloom and said: "Here's some advice: stick it in your ass." Then he started laughing for ten minutes straight. But that's to be expected from a life-time janitor: everything's a big old bathroom joke. After he died we threw him into the lawfirm sump pump as per his last request.

"There goes a man," my father said, by way of eulogy, "who could make a urinal squeal with delight..." I admit to shedding a manly tear or two.

Twenty Words for Free Lovin'

Fred walked back to his bunk with Margot on his mind. He thought of her bedroom; the white-and-pink bed sheets spread across the bed, the sweet-smelling candle burning on the windowsill, her naked body hidden by her long blonde hair.

In her last letter, sent two months ago, she promised to be waiting for him when he pulled his fishing schooner, *The Margot*, into dock. He took the tacked-up letter from the wall near the bunk bed:

Dear Freddy,

I think of you every day at least a couple of times. Thinking of you all alone on the ship makes me want to be with you so bad. I think of rubbing you and being with you. You probably want me so bad. All you got is those stinky fish (haha)

Mrs. Doleg says it's like when her ex-husband was in jail. After his three years, he was crazy for sex when he got back, like a rutting bull. She said you'll be a maniac for my sweet honey love. Sweety-pie, I'm gonna fuck your brains out. You earned it.

It's kinda lonely here, too. I end up going dancing with Barbara Ann and Nora Lee pretty much every night. All these guys get up on me and I'm so horny baby. (you better hurry…) Then I get back and the house is so empty. It's definitely much cleaner than when you were here. But then I think about having sex with you and being with you. Fishing is such a shitty life for people to be together. Anyway, I'll pick you up when you get home.

Love,
Margot

Fred took out the worn pornographic picture from his wallet and overwhelming love filled his chest. Margot wore only a tight denim vest and straddled his Hyundai motorbike, her chest thrown forward, red lips pouting, one almond-shaped eye winking alluringly. What a woman! If ever a man got suckered into marriage, this was the one. Fred was proud to have shown the picture to the rest of the *Margot* fishing crew.

Fred put the letter and picture back in his stack of papers, which included an article his father had written for the *Gazette* on car-engine repair, a picture of his dog, Cap'n, and a shiny rock he had found on a Haitian beach, and shoved the pile into a heavy jute gunny sack. He pictured Margot standing at the dock with her hands clasped together and tears streaming down her face. Once docked, he would take her roughly by the waist and dip her low and kiss her like the couples on the covers of the trashy novels that she read, *Raging Love. Eternal Romance.* Fred thought, *Doin' it on a Hyundai.*

Fred wondered if he had made a mistake thinking of Margot so much while he was away. He hoped the balance of power hadn't shifted. His dad had always told him that you can't think of the woman too much while you're out at sea or she'll know she got you. But Fred felt he could trust Margot, that he had to be able to trust her, if he was having all these girlie thoughts of marriage.

Anyway, he would take her straight home once he docked and have her get the bedroom ready while he showered. She would know who was in charge. As land came into view, Fred thought *Shit, I'm gonna give it to her. Make her cry with all the romantic things I'm gonna say.* Fred would see to it that she never went dancing again. He'd make her scream to the Lord above in apology for that line in the letter about *better hurry.*

Fred hastily stuffed his clothes into the gunny sack, dirty and clean together. He took out a romantic poem from *Romeo and Juliet* he'd been memorizing:

> *My bounty is as boundless as the sea,*
> *My love as deep; the more I give to thee,*
> *The more I have, for both are infinite.*

He read the lines over and then tested himself: "My bounty is as boundless as the sea. My love as," he cheated a look, "… deep." He hid the paper behind his back, "the more I give to thee, the more I have to thee, for both are finished." He took the poem out and checked. Close enough.

When he pulled the *Margot* into harbor it was about four in the afternoon and the pier was empty save for one small fishing boat with two old men sharing a pipe. The sky was pale and yellowish and a cold pier wind swirled from the water. Though Fred wondered where in the hell Margot was, he was happy to be back, relieved to put foot on solid ground. He secured the boat to the moor and looked up to see a woman from far off wearing faded denim shorts, a red halter top, and swinging her ass with each step side-to-side like a celebrity duck.

Margot.

Fred felt his face flush and silly joy tear through his chest. He jumped up and began jogging down the pier to greet her. He recited the memorized Shakespeare lines in his head. As he got closer he noticed a man walking alongside her. It was Gardiner the mechanic from Noken Street, Margot's old boyfriend. Fred slowed to a walk. Something wasn't right. Margot waved without concern, her broad face smiling pleasantly.

"Hey Freddy."

Gardiner grabbed his hand and shook, "Freddy, man, we're glad you're back."

Margot snapped her gum. "You remember Gardiner."

Fred's temper roared, "Yeah, of course I remember him. I kicked his ass in Ricky's Bar a year ago!"

"No hard feelings, dude." Gardiner eyed Fred's boat. He took out a cigarette and stepped towards the *Margot*.

Margot crossed her arms, "Well, me and him got back together two days ago."

"What! Two days ago!" Fred took a step forward and cocked his arm for a punch. "I'll kill him!" Gardiner flinched and fell on his backside.

Margot slapped Fred across the face. "Don't be an animal."

Fred rubbed his stinging cheek, "Margot, I thought we were together."

"I got tired of waiting for you." She wrinkled her nose. "God you smell..."

"You couldn't wait two more days?"

She snapped her gum a number of times with an open mouth and leaned forward. Her bosoms pushed against each other.

"No."

Fred fought to control his sadness. He could almost cry at the way Margot was treating him.

"I don't like people taking me for granted," Margot said, "I'm not a little girl." She had her hands on her hips and a take-me-serious look of a little girl.

"Yeah," Gardiner said, "We've been waiting for the boat." He let go of Margot and took a joyous leap into the *Margot*. "Yee-*hah*!" he exclaimed.

"Anyway we started doing each other the day you left," Margot shook her head and smiled towards the boat, distracted by Gardiner's antics. He was high-stepping on the deck with a mop across his shoulder like a Broadway-musical sailor. Fred stared at Margot and tried to interpret what was happening. He had planned on getting married but now everything was fucked-up. Margot smiled at Gardiner and brushed past Fred.

Fred grabbed her shoulder. "Hey," he forced back tears, "What's going on here?"

"Listen," she exhaled and explained, "Me and Gardiner have got something special. Something me and you don't have."

"You don't *remember*. You forget what we had."

"It doesn't matter anyway," her voice was shrill, "Me and Gardiner have an open relationship. Like the Eskimos. That's where we're going."

"What?"

"We're going to the Eskimos. An Eskimo was here while you were on your fishing trip, even though I told you that fishing was no life for normal people, and anyway, he told us at the Community Center how Eskimo men and women share each other freely with others. They, like, make love all day long. *That's* true love. Gardiner understands because he was *here* when the Eskimo spoke, but *you* weren't so you don't know shit."

Fred reeled at what he was hearing, "That's not true love! That's crazy!"

"No, *you're* crazy, Freddy! You think you could own me, but you don't own me. That's not love, that's possession. But I'm not a possession!" she cried, "And I want lots of men to love me because I'm a person." She stomped up the gangplank.

As they were talking, Freddy suddenly noticed a line of people forming to get on the boat. They held sleeping bags and coolers under their arms.

He spun and looked his neighbor, Mr. Wallenstadt, in the eye, "Wallenstadt, what the hell is going on?"

"We're all going." Margot yelled from the deck of the boat, "Everyone's coming with us towards the Promised Land of free love."

"You tell him, sweetheart," Gardiner yelled, then grabbed old Mrs. Wallenstadt, and planted a fat kiss.

Fred craned his neck, looking for someone familiar in the crowd. He saw his neighbor, Mr. Smoker, looking punchy and drugged. He repeated Mr. Smoker's name three times before the man turned. The whole time Fred talked, Mr. Smoker looked towards the boat, an impatient and empty look on his face. Fred wondered if the Eskimo that visited the Community Center knew hypnosis, or black magic.

"Mr. Smoker, where in the Lord's name are you going?"

"I'm going to Alaska, young man. We was all waiting for you."

Fred was incredulous, "You're gonna get true love? You're an old man."

"They got this ground-up reindeer testicle up there," Smoker made a motion, grinding one hand into the other, "Keeps your Smoker poker young."

"Shit!" Fred exclaimed, "All you people are crazy."

He turned and picked out his parents in the growing line of Alaska-bound zombies. He loped over and grabbed their shoulders. They both had the same glazed look in their eyes as Mr. Smoker.

"Mom, Dad, don't tell me you're going too."

"We are," his father said with blank eyes. "We're goin' to Eskimo-land."

"I think it's technically called the Aleutian Islands." Fred's mother added.

"We're gonna smoke us some canoes." His father chuckled and galloped onto the boat.

"What the hell is he talking about, Mom? What the hell is going on?"

Mrs. Yeatman took the cigarette from her mouth and blew a stream of smoke, "Your father seems to think that our sex life isn't so hot anymore."

Fred tripped over a pier-moor and fell on his left ear. His mother stepped over him and continued, "We're gonna learn from the Eskimos about boundless love. The whole town is going. You should go too."

"I'm not going to Alaska," Fred insisted face down.

His mom turned and shuffled up the gangplank, "Well, don't say you weren't invited. Not like Willie Tooman's eight-year-old birthday party. I never heard the end of *that*."

Fred stood up and rubbed his swollen ear. "To hell with them."

He walked into town. There was a traffic jam on Main Street with cars jostling, honking, and bumping.

As Fred walked by, he looked inside the back seat of a car and saw two kids wearing bathing suits and fighting with each other.

The father of the children yelled out the window, "Get outta the way! I gotta get to Lu-Lu land befores all the free love is gave away."

The mother shoved her head out of the passenger side window, "Get outta the goddamn way you slow bastards! I gotta get rid o' this sack of shit and get me a real man! An Eskimo man!"

An hour later, the streets were absolutely desolate. Everyone in town, it seemed to Fred, had left for Alaska. He could not believe how big and empty everything was.

He walked through the tree-shaded park, down the crumbling concrete steps, into the wide open clearing of the strip mall parking lot, where the kids at the high school used to make out with girls. He thought of Margot and how she gave it up to him there on their first date. *That* free love was true love; as far as Fred was concerned there was no other kind.

Across the strip mall lot, almost a football field away, a yellow plastic bag turned over and over in the light wind. Except for the crunchy whispers of the bag, Fred heard nothing. He cupped his hands around his mouth and yelled as loud as he could:

"Hullo!"

He waited for an answer. Nothing.

He walked across the gravel parking lot and made a game of stepping over the yellow painted lines. When he got to the middle of the lot he looked up and yelled again, "Hullo!" Again there was no response. He broke into a full speed run towards the FoodMart supermarket. He reached the automatic doors and was surprised to find a girl staring at him. She was thin and blonde and wore a FoodMart uniform.

"I heard you yelling," the girl said.

"Yeah, *so*?"

"So, where is everybody? I was taking a smoking break and then everybody was gone. I can't believe I have to work night shift."

"They all went to Alaska." Fred pushed past her and headed towards the frozen food section. He felt like eating a box of frozen hors d'oeurves.

The girl found Fred by the microwave. She had fudge stains all over her shirt. Her nametag read *Clarissa*.

"Do you think I should call my friends from the other

county?"

Fred shoved a hot cross bun in his mouth. "No, less food for us. If we're careful we'll never have to buy food again."

"The freezer's off, we have to eat all this ice cream right now."

Fred nodded and followed the girl outside. She sat on the bench in front of the store. She had three expensive French ice cream cakes in front of her. The one on her lap she cut into rectangular portions using a plastic spoon from the salad bar.

"Don't you think it's kinda freaky?"

Fred looked out over the empty parking lot. He concentrated on the noiseless background and the absence of cars whizzing by or people rushing past. "I don't really care if people are around or not around. I don't really care about anything." He stood up. "I'm gonna go for a walk for a while. I kinda want to be alone so I'm not going to ask you to come with."

"OK." She was spooning a fallen blob of ice cream off her lap. "I'll make steaks later if you want."

"Maybe."

"How will I get through to you? You want to take my phone number?"

"No, just yell."

As Fred walked up the stairs he heard her cry out, "Hey!"

He turned to find an incredulous look on her face. She ran to the stairs with the cake balanced on her upturned hand like a waitress holding a restaurant order.

"You think all the houses are empty? I mean we could break in, you know, if you want, and take all their rich stuff." She spun the plastic spoon in the air. "Their jewelry-like."

They broke into the first house in the rich part of town. Clarissa rifled through the fridge. Fred came down the stairs carrying a stuffed moose head.

"It's a shame all this food is going to spoil. What a waste."

He sat at the rich people's kitchen table and drank a rootbeer. He pretended the house belonged to him.

"Look—" she took out a long pink slab from the freezer, "—shark steak."

Later, Fred fried the shark. Clarissa came downstairs wearing three pairs of obese-women's underwear and a gigantic bra over her FoodMart uniform. She put her hand on her waist and stuck her hip out, "Does this turn you on? Let's me and you have some home-style Alaska sex."

Fred turned the steak in the frying pan.

"Come on, baby," she persisted, "I got some sealskin oil. I'll find us some blubber." She brought her pursed lips right up close to Fred and breathed seductively into his face, "*Hot... Wet... Blub... Ber.*" Fred pushed her away and she fell backwards over the stuffed moose head.

"I'm gonna throw up if you keep up with that talk."

Clarissa laughed wildly from the floor.

Fred stepped over her, "You crazy fucked-up chicks."

After eating, they went to the house next door. Hi-YA! Fred knocked the door down with a leaping roundhouse kick. An old lady was sitting in a rocking chair in the hallway. Fred yelped.

"Get the police!" the old lady yelled.

"I am the police," he answered.

"Oh."

"We were just checking out if you had enough… shark steaks." He audibly gulped.

"Slick," Clarissa whispered behind him. She was still wearing the oversized underwear.

"Why is it so quiet?" The old lady lifted herself out of her afghan-draped chair and toddled to the window, "Where are all

Twenty Words For Free Lovin'

the children?"

Clarissa stepped forward. "This is Heaven. You made it to Heaven…"

"Oh, that's fantastic. You know, something felt odd and I wondered…"

"Yeah, you were on the border there. Heaven-Hell-Heaven-Hell. But Gabriel, here—" she turned and pinched Fred's cheek "—got you in. He's been keeping an eye on you."

"I thought he was the police?"

"He's the angel police," Clarissa replied. Fred grimaced.

The old lady began searching around the coffee table. She suddenly cackled, "I was just about to take my pills. But that seems pretty silly now that I'm dead."

Clarissa guffawed like a clown, "Guh-*huh*. It sure does." She bounded out the front door.

Fred walked outside and found her lying in the street.

"What do you want to do now?"

Clarissa jumped and ran back inside. She returned thirty seconds later.

"I told her I was a different angel and she still had to take her pills in Heaven."

Fred lay down in the center of the street. "That was nice of you," he said, "You're a goddamn saint."

Clarissa lay down next to him. "Thanks, Gabe. That means a lot."

Fred was sitting on a swing in the park listening to Clarissa sing television show theme songs when people started returning from Alaska. His parents hopped out of the Gibson's minivan.

His mom called from the sidewalk, "Hello, son!"

Clarissa struggled out of the giant underwear. Fred stood from the swing and called back, "What happened?"

"We got to about Vikings-land…" his father began.

"—Nova Scotia, dear," Fred's mother corrected. "We got up there and then your father wanted to see his TV show. We didn't realize it's such a long trip. Alaska is not in the continental United States, you know."

Clarissa sat in the seesaw wearing her FoodMart uniform. She began singing again.

"Who's that?" his father asked, "Your new chick? She's not as hot as Margot."

Clarissa stopped singing and walked over. Fred's mother gave her a hug.

"Hello, dear. I'm Mrs. Yeatman, Fred's mother. Would you like to join us for dinner?"

"No thanks. Fred made shark and I brought ice cream."

"Oh, how nice."

" 'Scuse me," Fred's father walked away, "I gotta get to the TV. Be careful of Mrs. Dalloways. She got left behind and we saw her riding down the street on her dog, singin' about children taking pills in Heaven or some such nonsense..."

Fred sat on the bench next to Clarissa. "Man, I liked it better when everybody was gone."

"Yeah, me too. Anyway, I gotta get back to FoodMart. Seeya."

Fred returned to the pier. The *Margot* swayed in the soft breeze. As he approached the fishing schooner, Fred thought about changing the name to *Clarissa*. Suddenly, Gardiner appeared on the ship deck and started blubbering: "You gotta hear this Fred: my dick froze when we got to Canada. Then Margot fell in love with this guy because he had the same last name as her. She liked that she didn't have to get her driver's license changed. We didn't get past Toronto. She's gonna marry him, so I guess I'm dumped like you, Freddy! Ha, ha, we both got nothing. We're really in the same boat."

Fred grabbed Gardiner's overalls and hauled him onto the dock. "Get out of my face before I kill you."

Gardiner freed himself, "Let's me and you take a trip to Alaska, Freddy, and get us some free love."

"No." Fred untied the boat, got in, and started the motor.

"C'mon, Freddy," he pleaded. He dropped to his knees and covered his face with his hands. He was crying as Fred pulled away from the pier. "All's I wanted was Margot plus some free lovin'. I don't understand what happened." Gardiner bawled, "Margot! Freeeeeeeeee lovin!"

Notebook #14

—Oil bike hinges. Get Phil to prepare roller skates and duffel bag. Do test run Monday to see if street speed between bike and roller-skates is highly variable. Explain to Phil that he can't allow bag to drag. In preparation make Phil do sit-ups (20+) and pushups (30+). Zip and lock woman. Case closed.

—Fisherman's maxim in effect: throw small ones back. Complete list of how to judge appropriate level of attractiveness:
1. Youthfulness and ability to keep youthfulness. (Is wisdom featured in appearances?)
2. Eyes are most important. (Brown versus green versus unsettling gold)
3. Legs or boobs. Must one choose? (Conduct poll at chess club)
4. Big mouth and bigger teeth, no explanation necessary.

—After large haul, grill her in the living room. Who cooks! How much does your hair treatment cost! Does your underwear have printed on it the days of the week? The months of the year? The years of the Millennium?

—Is there attractiveness in attitude? Funny girls have funny sex? Scary girls have scary sex?

—Recall college experiences, re-read notebook #12. Valentine's Day Party, under the bed looking for lost panties. Horse-faced girl named Susan and your handsome roommate, Foster. Explanation for this otherwise aesthetically disparate pairing: Foster, full of ale, is not in a discriminate state of mind. Foster pauses foreplay to urinate. Susan calls her friend on the cellphone: "I can't believe I'm getting felt up by a hot guy!" Foster returns only to fall asleep. The phone vibrates. "I can't. I don't want to wake him up." In the mirror I see Susan's tongue hang from the side of her mouth. "His pants are at his knees! I'm in Heaven!"

—Under bed, panties in hand, I think: Woe is the female gender! Too stupid to be alive! Certain extinction!

—Education is key to sorry disrepair. Chain her to the kitchen sink with just enough slack to reach the stovetop and she'll write the next great work of literary philosophy. Write write write. When she hesitates, and says "I'm anxious, I'm not sure I've had enough babies," I'll tell her, "Don't be a boob."

>**boob**[1]
[Slang] a stupid or foolish person

—I repeat, "Don't be a boob. Don't you know that women won't even have babies in a hundred years? Everything in a lab; harvesting eggs and so forth. Yay for the progress of art!

—Are woman better off without their monthlies? (Ask the women you know: Mother, Grandma, Mrs. Zulchek)

—Scratch that! Forget education. Plan on the woman being unteachable. Look for Muses. Someone quiet and pretty who makes good scrambled eggs. Someone who says the word *tushy* with dignity.

—No. Scratch again. Shoot for woman-as-motivation. Concentrate on discovering hidden pockets of cruelty, sagging writing career needs jumpstart. She'll teach focus on the desperation of human cause, psychological warfare of sex withheld, teased, then glory and sniveling gratitude. Begin heroin diet. Find salty rocks at spiritual nadir and make a bed. Find woman who beats you with Personal Computer equipment and helps plans for dramatic suicide attempt (Ask FatPhil for video recorder).

Write the worst stories:
  1. A baby dying.
  2. An old man dying.
  3. A beautiful young mother, so needed at home by her young children, and she is dying.

—Must marry a young dying mother. Now is the time! Beautiful: luminescent skin, pale as rainchoked dawn, loose skirt, soft voice, gentle as a sickly baby's cough. She worries for her four-year-old son, a religious genius, he dispenses Ghandian wisdom. Could he be easier to love? What a woman! So unselfish! Sing to her as she dies.

In Heaven there's a baby.
He loves you he loves you
In Heaven there's a horsie.
He loves you.

—Have a dying baby with her. Make a movie exactly as long as the dying baby lives. Do it now! FatPhil! Where is FatPhil and his video recorder! My time is short. I know I will die tomorrow.

—Where is woman to manage my talent! Brain loses precious pieces of creativity, color-washed, spewed to acedic elements. No time for redirection of sexual imperative. Once again, time eludes, pall descends. The moment asserts:

—Feeling of controllessness, of barely suppressed lunacy. The heart swells with mind's madness and palpitates irregularly with consumption of own blood. This is the life bequeathed, alone and unshared. No escape, we must face the wall that God made: There is no expression or narrative to sum up the human condition.

Cyrus's Revelation

Cyrus sits in front of his new mail-order computer. The monitor lights his face yellow. He is a big man, over six-foot-two, 240 pounds, with thick black hair, four days of scruffy beard, and acne scars in his cheekpits. He wears blue jeans and a red-and-black checkerboard flannel shirt over white thermals.

He yells to his wife who is at the stove in the kitchen of their trailer, "Hey, Willie Mae, how does ya spell pertend?"

"Huh? Cyrus. I'm feedin' the kids."

"Yeah, but how does ya spell pertend?"

"I'll only tell you if you're not pertending yer a lesbian."

"I ain't. It's for finding work."

"Alright. P!-E!-R!-T!-E!-N!-D!"

Cyrus snickers and types into the computer: *Let's pertend we're rubbing each others pooders!*

The other user in the private chatroom writes back: *We're not pertending, we really are! I love your confidant feminine hands on my pooder.*

"Oh Gawd," Cyrus exclaims in ecstasy. He digs his hand into his pants.

His wife, Willie Mae, suddenly appears in their bedroom closet. She wipes her hands on a dishtowel. She is thin with work-hardened hands. A blond permanent, disobedient of gravity, wiggles at the top of her head like a mold of Jell-o.

"What kind of work you looking at?" she asks, "I don't know no kind of work you needs to pertend for, 'cept bein' an actor or salesman."

"Damn you woman!" Cyrus extracts his hand from his pants, "Cain't a man have privercy in his own closet."

"What was you doin'?" she asks defiantly, "You was pertendin' you was a lesbian again! Wasn't you? You lyin' bastard!"

Willie Mae runs into the kitchen and yells to their children, Ronald Lee, age 8, and Sylvania, age 4, "Your father's a lesbian, kids! Its time we moved out so's he don't have to pertend no more!"

Ronald Lee begins crying. Cyrus jumps from his plastic lawn chair and rumbles into the kitchen.

"Now listen here, woman." He raises his finger, "I ain't no lesbian. I might be a woman stuck in a man's body but you is still my family and this here is still my trailer."

"Don't wave that finger at me, mister," Willie Mae yells back. "God only knows the women you stuck her into, you dirty dyke! Running around behind my back like you is."

Cyrus's forehead compacts above his eyes and his nostrils flare into two wide hoops. "Now listen here, Willie Mae, I been here ever night of the week and you knows that."

"Yeah, running loose in those chatrooms. Same thing as monkey business."

"Willie Mae, you listen up now, I been doin' some reading…"

"Oh no," Willie Mae raises her hands, as if to extract herself from the conversation. She begins clearing the table, "Kids, your father been doin' some reading. What happens when dear old dad does some reading?"

Sylvania yells, "Grandma dies!"

"Yu-huh, you got it little missy."

Cyrus frowns at his daughter, "Now, hey, that was all well-conceived. I don't see why we need pay for brand name botulism when we can grow it ourselves from home store."

"Cyrus—if you still keeping that *man* name—Grandma's face was twitching even as she lay a'carcass in the grave."

Sylvania yells, "She look a skeery clown!"

Ronald Lee suddenly perks up, "Do you know what she said?"

Sylvania yells, "Don't say it!"

"She said—" Sylvania screams and plugs fingers into her ears, "—the worms are in my face!" Ronald Lee smiles broadly.

"Or what about Ronald Lee's braces?"

The boy slouches in his chair and pushes his plate of creamed corn and oatmeal away.

"Son, those adult teeth'll come in any day now. Nothing wrong with dentures. Ronald Reagan had dentures for thirty year."

Willie Mae stands with her hand on her cocked hip, "Or what about that reading you did on 'lectronics. I don't know how that talking clock of yours learned all those filthy words. I almost got arrested."

"But listen," His voice was shrill with explanation, "I been doin' some reading and there's a seventy-percent chance you is bi-sekshul, too."

"Well, I don't know what you're getting at Cyrus Waltrip Bushgarden but I ain't doin' no monkey business if that's where you're anglin'."

"No monkey business. I just wanted to do the bump-and-run with your panties on my head. Is that too much to ask?"

"That's it? But Cyrus, we ain't done the bump-and-run for ten year now."

"That's all I want. I knows you still got it in you."

"You promise that's all?"

Cyrus's Revelation   141

"Promise."

"Well, that's OK from my side," Willie Mae threw the dishtowel in the sink and walked past Cyrus into the bedroom; she gave him a playful bump with her negligible hip.

"But I ain't putting *your* underwear on my head." She glowered at him so he knew she meant business. "Even if they inside out."

The Robot Garden

The year was 43-KN-1982 and the entire surface of the planet Earth was covered with artificial materials. It was a big rotating ball made of gleaming iron skyscrapers, glass supersonic traveling tubes and clear plastic skyboat speedways.

The thing which nowadays we call *Nature* no longer existed. Nostalgically walking through an acre of green plant life in the future could only be experienced for a small fee on the holovision set; but the ancient *holo-forest* was always shown to be smelly and disagreeable with no good spots to go to the bathroom or find a tasty Porridge-Shake. What's most important for you to know is that even though it was the future and everything was different, there were still normal people like you and me.

Two people that were normal were Jipple and Muffsack. They loved to sit around all day long and play videogames instead of doing their schoolwork. Neither of them had girlfriends, and both of their mothers thought they spent too much of their free time in their Automatic Simulation Stimulation Booth.

One time Jipple's mother, Mrs. Lipnip, said to him in the kitchen, "What do you *do*, anyway, in that Automatic Simulation Stimulation Booth?"

Jipple was standing on a FutureChair fixing an Automatic SuperLightbulb and he immediately fell on the floor, "You mean the ASS-Booth?" he asked embarrassedly.

Mrs. Lipnip raised her eyebrows and crossed her arms. Muffsack was digging through the Automatic Food Processor looking for Pre-Chewed food and he started laughing. He knew that, like him, Jipple spent his time in the Booth talking to animate and highly attractive robot girls.

"Uh—," Jipple explained as he dusted himself off, "—I do my homework."

Jipple's mother, a dense woman, gave him a sideways glance. "Wait a second," she said, "There's no such thing as homework anymore. This is the future. They just put the information straight into your head."

As Jipple sputtered to explain, Muffsack chortled silently and made lewd gesticulations behind Mrs. Lipnip's back, as if he was having sex with a super hot robotgirl.

"What are you laughing at, you oil can douche bag," Jipple yelled at Muffsack, "Everyone knows *you're* in love with Flirty Metalboobs."

"The six p.m. newscaster on Channel Fourteen-Thirty-Seven?" Mrs. Lipnip giggled, "I thought that was a man."

"God, Mom," Jipple blushed with embarrassment, "her *name* is Metalboobs for godsakes."

"I don't know." Mrs. Lipnip put a hand to her mouth, "She has a very deep voice."

"C'mon, let's go, Muffsack." Jipple grabbed his friend by the shirt and stalked into the TV room. "I think my mom is future-retarded."

He turned on the TV to Channel Fourteen-Thirty-Seven. The six p.m. news was starting.

Flirty Metalboobs was wearing a low-cut elastic shirt, and her metal boobs looked fierce and uncompromising.

"Turn it up." Muffsack jumped on the couch.

Flirty turned in her seat behind the newsdesk and arranged some blank pieces of papers with her robotic claws. She began the newscast in her signature officious voice:

"The Emperor of the Earth, SunPenis MoonVagina, is dead. It is a very sad day for men and robots alike even though he was a purely ornamental diplomat and did nothing important. At the end of his life, when he was losing his mind, he started a rumor that there was a mystical Emperor's Garden of Nature somewhere on Earth with a secret microchip that can turn robots into humans. Other than that he was just a regular worthless old man.

The government of Earth has decided that Emperors are boring and instead of finding a replacement Emperor, some other institution will be set up, but no one yet knows what. You'll have to wait until next Tuesday to see if you have to vote or perhaps be killed for your beliefs. Also there's a chance that the robots will take over the world. Now here's Chester Goldnuts with the weather.

"I thought there was no such thing as weather anymore," Muffsack said and took a drink from his Porridge-Shake.

"Did you hear what she said about the Emperor's garden? That's so weird."

"I don't know," Muffsack said. Both boys sat in silence for a moment and then Muffsack spoke up, "...She does kind of have a deep voice."

Jipple frowned at Muffsack, "So you don't love her anymore just because of what my mom said?"

"Well," Muffsack looked at his hands with embarrassment, "maybe it's time I grew up. She's a robot, y'know. A famous robot. The chances of something happening are so small."

"Oh, shut up," Jipple said, "You're losing your mind. Let's play videogames."

The boys started playing their favorite videogame which was called *When I Take Over the World, You'll Be My Punching Bitch.*

Both of them were in their videogame-playing trance when, all of a sudden, on the 131st level, a door opened up in the hallway of the SuperCastle into a secret board called "The Emperor's Mystical Garden." Jipple pressed the MAP button on the videogame controller and searched through the landscape layout of the level. "That looks familiar," he told Muffsack

"*That* road," Muffsack took the porridge straw away from his mouth and pointed at the holovision screen, "is the one me and my dad take to PlastoVille to get our skyboat wings rotated. What's it doing in a videogame?"

"Yeah, yeah," Jipple was getting very excited and he jumped up onto the couch knocking over Muffsack's Porridge-Shake, "When our family became futureCommunists we had to march on that road. I remember now."

Soon the boys finished the videogame board. They reached the center of the garden where they retrieved a small microchip embedded in the cliff-face. The microchip had the power to transform any robot in the world into a human.

"That was a great videogame," Muffsack said, "I just can't figure out why they used a real road."

"I think they did it on purpose," Jipple answered.

"Do you think that's the way to the Emperor's Mystical Garden? The real garden?"

"It's got to be," Jipple said with confidence. He turned to Muffsack, "We're supposed to find that Secret Garden. I *know* we are. Don't you see, they left this secret videogame board as a clue! For us!"

He clenched his fist, "We've got to find the SunPenis MoonVagina Mystical Garden. It's our journey." Jipple went into a reverie and a smile spilled across his face, "I can't believe that fate would give us such a special purpose. And I've never even seen real Nature. I wonder what it's like."

"Well, OK," Muffsack began to tremble. Jipple's excitement

made him nervous, "If we're gonna go on a scavenger hunt to find Nature maybe I should go to the bathroom and pack some extra Porridge-Shakes."

"Fine," Jipple passionately threw his hand towards the door, "But rain or shine we leave in two hours."

Jipple and Muffsack began walking to the skybus station and they felt great. It was very exciting for them to find a secret adventure and to be following it out. And neither of them had ever seen the thing called *Nature* since the surface of the entire Earth was covered with metal, plastic and glass. Muffsack was less enthusiastic, seeing as how Porridge-Shakes were a mainstay of his diet and Nature didn't promise easy access, but Jipple had a feeling, a *future* feeling, that it might be the most magical day of their lives.

Real Nature, he thought as they boarded their twelve-hour skybus ride, *I bet it smells great.*

After the second skybus transfer, Muffsack took out a copy of the videogame map they had brought with them.

"It says there's a grotto of hobbits...," Muffsack pointed at the map, "here... and a coven of witches right before the forest. I think we need to know magic to get through there."

"Magic!" Jipple sputtered and fell into the aisle. A robo-stewardess came running over with a glass of water. Jipple calmed himself,

"Magic! This is the future, Muffsack. That's crazy. There is no such thing as magic anymore."

"I think," Muffsack replied with a new look of intensity, "That the magic is in us already."

"You mean—"

"Yes. When we need it, it will come forward." Muffsack sat back to study the map.

"Wow." Jipple folded the vomit bag into a paper airplane

and thought, *I didn't realize Muffsack was so wise.* He wondered if it felt really great when the magic from inside came forward. Would it be like, or unlike, when he laid down the perfect pick-up line on a robotgirl in the ASS-Booth?

Soon they got off the plane and began to walk. They saw real trees and bushes from far off, and began to run towards it. It was very exciting because they had actually found what they were looking for. Then they realized that they were coming up quickly on a coven of witches they recognized from the videogame and Muffsack immediately got into a meditative trance in order to make proper battle. Jipple was very impressed.

"Are you ready yet?" Jipple asked.

Muffsack took a swig of Porridge for extra energy.

"OK," he said, and they cautiously approached the witches.

But then they crossed the valley and all the witches turned out to be automatic robo-witches, not very scary at all, and no magic was necessary. Muffsack was deeply disappointed and he began to cry.

"I really felt like there is magic inside me," he explained to Jipple, "Special magic that I knew would come out when we needed it. I knew I would save the day. Now the magic is stuck inside me and I feel like shit."

"It's probably just gas," Jipple offered.

Muffsack slumped and walked past the ugliest robo-witch. He gave it a kick in the leg.

"Magic gas," he said sadly.

They continued walking. The map brought them to a small building with curved arches above the door. Then it brought them to a climbing sculpture, a gigantic unused mini-mall, and a gold-plated fountain that spewed the finest Porridge-Shake a hundred feet into the air.

"I think we're on the right track," Muffsack said as he dipped his hand into the Porridge Basin and filled his mouth. He smiled at Jipple, "It's good."

Then they finally arrived at the forest. It was really beautiful, nothing like the holovision had said. Plenty of places to go to the bathroom, plenty of places to drink your fill of delicious natural-spring Porridge.

"A forest still alive!" Jipple exclaimed. He lay on a bed of pine needles that smelled more natural then even the most natural holovision recreation. It was the happiest moment he could remember.

"Nature is pure magic," Muffsack said, "I knew it all along." He turned in circles on the bed of pineneedles, face and arms held to the shaded sky. He gazed with wonder at all the Nature.

There were trees satiny with moss and leafy ferns. It was holy, holy ground. Elves and sprites and satyrs and nymphs sprang from algaed ponds and gnarled tree roots and caves embedded in the hilltops. They offered Jipple and Muffsack Porridge-cakes and tasty Porridge biscuits and danced in magic circles around the two visitors singing, "Tra-la, tra-la, welcome to the magic forest." The boys erupted into fits of giggles of delight. They had never felt so human in all their lives.

But then, anyway, at the end of the story, it turned out that Jipple and Muffsack were just robots themselves—trend robots—the stupidest robots that there are. And even though they could talk and walk they were just following their trendy programming.

Later that day, they met ten thousand other trend robot kids in the garden that had watched the very same Flirty MetalBoobs Holovision newscast that mentioned the Emperor's Mystical Garden and played the very same videogame that had the secret map of the Garden. It was all a big test by the National Robotic

Association to make sure the circuits of the robots, the trend robots, didn't get rusty.

Soon all the robots were programmed to go home. "I feel like we should go home," Jipple said with no actual thought involved and all the trend robots agreed, agreed, that is, in purely binary computer code. Then, a few years later, it became trendy for all those robots to get married and have children and to love the children and they all did it because their programming said so. Then it became trendy to stop loving the children and they all immediately stopped.

Mojave

I live in Iceberg, Nevada, the godforsaken desert, an hour from New Mexico state line. There's no humans here, only shades of wasted wanderers. All movement's a sort of scurrying. The sun punishes the overbaked earth. At midday the eyes are beguiled of common sense. Scenery wobbles like a mirage in convection, visions of water on the flat plain. The heat is of a demoralizing breed; it compels philosophy: What's real?

Inside, I'm standing by the air conditioner with a beer from the freezer against my forehead looking out my trailer window. The juiceless stones, the rocky hills like piles of black cinders. The sweat stains on my shirt are cold but it doesn't penetrate. Even when I wet my cheeks down. Even when I put my face against the unit.

They say to keep hydrated but I've drunk all the bottled water months ago. Now all I've got is claypots that I truck in from Sante Fe full of brackish wellwater. The pots are decorated with natural plant dye by the feeble hands of third-world children and old women who surely shared dysentery germs into their craftwork. I bought each pot for a dollar at the side of the highway. I can taste the protozoa when I drink, as greasy as pond scum in my dry throat. In the water, I see cells grow before my eyes: organisms the size of pinheads sprout into tadpole-like flagellates, which unfold into fully-animate creatures the size and shape of shell-less corkscrew snails. I imagine them making a home in my belly, reproducing, overflowing until I burst with invertebrate parasite life.

Not quite semen. But you take what you can get.

The desert reminds daily how the human is only a short stop on the train of life. Eventually, nature has its way.

Only a thinking mind could have created this lunacy, this hazy waking dream. Sometimes I wonder: have I made these circumstances? And why would I impose impotency? What perverted desire am I attempting to excavate? The inside and the outside seem too congruous, it confuses.

Is it my obsession with misfortune or the dry silo of old age? They always said I think too much, talk too much. Words, words, words only serve to confuse. It seems, as a principle, I encourage confusion—confusion and delusion. But I never guessed it would be my sowing equipment. It all comes full circle in that way because knowledge is a sort of impotence. And impotence gives a privileged view of knowledge. Either way, I should stop these thoughts and get out of here; it's all a form of madness. This is why I never get enough sleep.

Fuck. I can't even get a hard-on in this wilting heat. One can't live in this punishing world straight on, it beats down hard, it cudgels into a whimpering mass. If you stand up straight and throw your shoulders back it doesn't matter. Everything wilts in this carnal sun. Brutality rains. Brutality reigns.

There was a time I could welcome that punishment. But only a teenager has that masochistic thrust to defy God's displeasure. With age my delusions have grown subtler, quicker, more pathetic. Reliance on language stole my sex. All I want these days is to watch unchanging scenery in cool comfort with a beer in hand.

Steinbeck loved the desert, loved the idea of solitude:

"panting asthmatically, hermits of the early church piercing to infinity with unlittered minds. The great concepts of oneness and majestic order seem always to be born in the desert." But I don't buy it. That's over-Romanticized, overcooked imagining: Everything Ugly is Beautiful, Everything Full of Death is Really Full of Microscopic Life. It's all just dressed up optimism, offensive to the heart. Dali is more my type. He knew the brain is not very reliable. It's only a chilly breeze across an empty expanse with the face of a melted clock. When we do pierce the depths of space we do so temporarily. The fury that chokes up around this breach, that heals this breach, promises to close us out, if not only of what we have newly discovered but also what we have heretofore taken for granted. God makes no appearance in Dali's play. Unless the feeling of being pushed away is God's bitter finger, indistinguishable from the devil's snub.

   I've used each of this Service's girls numerous times, wresting from each of them enough sympathy for my predicament that no sexual tension could possibly exist. In my house, they are not prostitutes but friends I pay. I do suggest they enjoy lemonade in the nude but that is more a matter of aesthetics. It is, after all, too hot to move, too hot for sex, too hot to talk. We stew in our own juices, contemplating the distant desolate vulture calls.
   I won't bother owning up now to this most recent one. She'll find out soon enough. "Dearest, don't mate with me," would I say, "I breed dustbunnies, stillchildren. I store only white lifeless jelly-like masses, abortional stores..." I won't anymore stockpile discomfort for the sake of honesty. Hard days are best ridden out mildly paced.
   This is the second time this callgirl has come by and I ask her to use a straw to suck it straight out of the testicle sac; I've read the appendage resides at lower temperatures. The girl looks inside with a microscope (she was once a nursing student) and

gives me the bad news. She wears the same expression as the Las Vegas doctor who diagnosed my impotence: a messenger attempting to look sympathetic but secretly elated that a bad thing should happen to anyone but him. I look out my trailer window to the two yellow humps of mountains which boundary this section of the Mojave, one large and one small. Some wicked lizard pauses to gawk at me from the windowsill, then retreats to a shadowy corner. The floral constellation of acne stretching from cheek to chin momentarily vivifies a flicker of joy. "But no…" she whispers, she's wearing a tight nurse's outfit per the magazine advertisement, "…the heat's got there too. The sperms are cooked like a wad of boiled eggwhite. Too stringy for erotica." She flicks her short black bob from her pristine forehead, rocks backward on the balls of her feet, and stands from a kneeling position. Her skirt is absurdly short, surely a Halloween costume and not a medical professional's.

"Breakfast," I say brightly, optimistically farce-ing, before she can speak again. In the desert summer you take bad news with a short sigh, never long enough to waste mouth-moisture. Every subliming droplet is a treasure. That's a fact that even impotency doesn't change.

That reality removed a last pleasure from my life two years ago is no big surprise. I'll be fifty-five come July, and the joys I know are stripped thin. Since youth I expected only suffering, such is my constitution. Even in Michigan, my boyhood haven in the 60's, I believed there was nowhere to hide, no such thing as hiding at all. The fact that I ended up in Iceberg was inevitable. If it hadn't been a desert before I arrived, my presence would assuredly have transformed it.

I separate from my guest to look out the window. By the cactus, in the glare of the sun, a form reflects harshly. I see the shadow of an animal slither by, could be coyote, could be jackrabbit, could be human, all sufferers look the same. It moves away from a split-bellied carcass. A snack, sunlashed and cooking. The war of heat and dryness perpetuates.

I've realized in the course of my days that the shadow is the only real and sane animal. It won't look straight at the sun's all-conquering deathray, it knows to hide behind a sweating body. Near the skulking animal, steam quivers from the ground, from its origination in Hell. Even the ghost of water is looking for escape from Iceberg. The nurse-whore clears her throat and I remember to be embarrassed by indulgence: nothing's calmer than to be alone in another's presence.

You come out to this desert to die; it's no secret, this nurse-whore included. I've not met this girl before—she's new here—and god only knows what sent her staggering into Nowheresville and its ragtag community of professional dyers. Like stumbling on an unlucky charm, this town is equivalent to stepping in dogshit that no amount of wiping can remove. I guess she arrived for a landclaim at night; that's how most of us were tricked.

Night-times, the temperature flirts with ranges bearable to the human glandular system. The darkness doesn't proclaim quite distinctly how little there is to witness. The armored insects, beetles, ants and scorpions, court and play and eat and hate. Chilled and coiled, all is submerged into the soup of night. That's the difference between sterility and this desert. Once the sun is down the desert animals sanely creep and scatter from their caves to conduct life. Unlike my midsection, work gets done here by cool darkness.

Is it possible the nurse-whore caught news of the roaming sirens, the desert beauties, from faraway? Perhaps she was fooled by the song. These out-of-work jobless Mojavians, all searching in the tradition of Manifest Destiny, stalking that Dream of Conquest through the sagebrush. By roasted skeletonbones, painted blue by the moon, we join temporarily in anonymous one-ness, a short respite from solitude, in the gagging swallowing dark. At some point the song ends and we each go our own ways, pretending to be taking a casual midnight stroll, embarrassed to see our same sad situation reflected in another.

I could go on with Grecian allusions about this madness which sustains the routine of our miserable lives. It's a welcome madness is what I'm saying. But even that beautiful song is not worth the emptiness, the yearning mass of Iceberg. The uninitiated can't see how this is the edge of the world, its worthless corner, its dank airless armpit, its useless vacuum asshole.

My trailer lizard squats in the shadows and struggles mightily, bearing itself a new life from a womb of dead skin. While the girl is in the bathroom I collect the carapace with a pair of tweezers and put it on the shelf next to the crumbling, transparent snake and scorpion casings.

The toilet flushes.

"Whatchoo got there? Dead things?"

"Just empty skins."

She pokes a rattler and crisps flake to the table.

"They resemble life, suggest past life, but hold nothing but the form of life. It's just a shell."

She laughs brightly, "Oh, you old men."

I could almost abuse her. No one gets to the Iceberg desert by accident. New girl doesn't see what's abundantly clear, as clear as the summer air is dense. When she gives me my check-up I mercifully hold back my psychological diagnosis: "Darlin', you're here because all along you've been meaning to die…"

I've given second thought to the sirens of the cactus fields. In that collective delusion it's possible to believe for fleeting moments that it's not all worthless. Maybe this new nurse-whore heard the seductive call from outside, from another state, and came to confirm. Perhaps she hasn't come here to die; the sirens *are* powerful. Shaken from sleep as if by an earthquake, we somnambulate the ancient sands like love-struck zombies, forgetting our real-life physical lovers, the dream is so strong. Separate in our loneliness we stalk the night in search of the Company of Companies. Last night, as I shambled blindly in the unearthly glow of the moonlit wasteland, I think I remember her stalking alongside, groping spastically with that dire need of practiced Icebergians.

Does she hear the voice of boys, like I hear the naiad girls? I must find a way to ask. Do women fall in love with this dream like we do, like all these broken Iceberg men?

An indolent black cat, as unfriendly as a demon, sneaks around my trailer steps, wondering if I have foodscraps. It hisses and stares me down, evaluates my weakness before sauntering off. I haven't moved from the couch in three days. I'm glad no one is around. Other people have a way of making me feel guilty about loneliness.

The next day the isolation overtakes and I call the nurse-whore. She returns in the same costume and I provide her a frozen beer and a choice seat in front of the air conditioner fan. And this girl is ugly and pretty; ugly because she is too real, fleshy and discolored. And she is pretty, too, because even in her realness she is still unreal, untouchable, an angel torn from heaven and brought within touching distance. I sit at her side in a porch chair and smack the ventilator when it rattles with complaint. She sips at her beer and giggles. I try to look up her minuscule skirt with little luck; the informality of sharing the afternoon has made her coy and innocent and instantaneously beautiful. But I won't try to sleep with her. Why push the masculine posture when all parties are privy to the sham?

At this point, anyhow and ironically, she is more health care professional then sex partner. I learn her name is Danielle and during the hottest hour of the day, 1 p.m. to 2 p.m., I serve her Jack-and-lemonade with my sourest attitude. She is drawn to my pessimism as if she too wishes to learn a total absence of lust for life. When afternoon arrives, and the sky begins to glow with rosy palliation, she gives me a checkup as a matter of routine—just so I know a service was provided and money is expected to change hands. She smiles politely at my arousal, pushes the diversion away like a focused nurse.

I spend the entire night arranging and rearranging the dead reptile skins. I decide I will present Danielle with one. A gift. I find the dry husks fascinating, the way the yellow, delicate segments fit together, ugly and strange but perfectly connecting, like aliens made of vulnerable glass. I hope she appreciates how they are not just lifeless, not just dead, *more* than dead because of the empty suggestion. A gift: more dead than dead.

The next day, with my binoculars, I see Danielle enter Rocketboom's trailer. She wears black, a witch's costume, and I am inconsolably jealous. Rocketboom's a dangerous guy, I don't know his real name, but he speeds around Iceberg on his motorcycle (named Rocketboom) all day to stay cool. Outside his trailer is a patch of starveling corn and strips of drying jerky hanging from a clothesline.

I don't know where he gets the money for gas. I know, like the rest of us, he has no job. He did a tour of duty for the U.S. Army somewhere in Asia and I imagine he receives a pension. But the military messed him up. At night you can hear him punching holes in his trailer walls and taking potshots with his magnum at horned toads. Once I knocked on his door as a friendly gesture. Shirtless, with heavy metal music shaking the ground beneath the trailer, he waved a gun in my face. Now that I think of it I've *never* seen him with a shirt on.

As he accepts Danielle into his trailer, he wears no shirt. I feel Danielle is a traitor.

Like a mooning and lovestruck schoolboy I watch the trailer religiously for an hour, my eyes squinched together for a better view.

Suddenly, I hear a gunshot. I am outside moving fast. Danielle runs out screaming: "You crazy asshole!" I am embarrassed. I backtrack before she sees me. I would hate for her to ask, "And what exactly did you plan to do to Rocketboom?"

Later, I call the agency and ask for Danielle. When she comes over we don't speak. She has a black eye. I pay her nothing.

Amazingly enough I see Danielle go back to Rocketboom's trailer a few days later. I feel bereft. The kind of prostitute who finds some congruous justice in being smacked around. Terrible: to wallow in disrespect.

When she arrives later that afternoon, I feel I can't dwell on my daily portion and I tell her: "Get the hell out."

She slams the trailer door and marches towards the night. Clap–bang–clap, the rusty hinges scream like demons, the screen door exhales the rasp of a dying old maid. I hurt her feelings and I'm glad. I feel like a cuckold cheated of what's rightfully mine. I go to the door but I don't have strength to yell an apology. She disappears into the distance towards the brothel-trailer near the buzzard nests at the clifftop. Some distant animal whines and howls—one of those animal calls which symbolize something primal of the human condition—in the cactus growth over the far ridge; a coyote, wild dog, a wolf, some pained monster.

When the animal screams again, I shiver. What cruel evolution could have tortured the canine so? As she walks home she probably thinks: even the lonely old man cuts my visit short.

If she only knew. If I owned sufficient self-esteem I'd drown her in acceptance. But she has her youth and she knows. If I remind her, "You're beautiful," she instantly remembers that she is *too* beautiful for *me*. How twisted these love-less love affairs, how distantly they comment on our self-knowledge.

I look into the sheet of cheap aluminum-mapped glass that serves as the bathroom mirror in my trailer. You would think I was vain I spend so much time looking at my dappled twisted reflection. But I'm just trying to push for the soul of the matter; the convincing of *what is*. I've got no chance against a man like Rocketboom. I'm a manless man. It must be a sin to be too aware of your deficiencies. Simply put, god made it necessary for us to lie to ourselves. I repeat the words to myself, "you are impotent," but they lack conviction, the total despair yet refuses to fully settle.

But now, to my mind, suddenly dawned, as I look again in the mirror, an unconscious understanding: all along I've felt my sexual vitality might return should I find those dancing women, the midnight sirens. If they should exist, I've always reasoned, then surely they own magical elixirs and alchemical cure-alls. Simply one drop should restore all my life, my lust for life, which was owned confidently by the young man I once was. What to do with this dream now that I've isolated its untruth I do not know. Should I stop the dream of catching the uncatchable?

If I was dying I could look at myself in the mirror and say, "Buddy boy, you're dying," and never comprehend what I've said. Only the insane could be so frank. Likewise, I see only a handful of ladies over the course of the month. I don't leave home much and hunting the siren singing-grounds is excluded as sociability. Searching for those golden-throated beauties wreathed with crimson cactus flowers, hearing just over the next horizon the cool warble of flutes, the pleasing vibration of harps, steals all human attention. No one speaks at night when stalking the circle-dancers. It is understood that there is a place of exuberance where there exists no clothes, and they drink only the coolest most delicious beer. Walk lightly, do not even whisper, for the dream beckons, the dream makes the world good, the dream must not be shared.

Perhaps part of the singing nymphs allure is the justified neglect of fellow man. These days, a shuffle through the thin hallway of my trailer serves as exercise. Truthfully, I can't even make it to the Sante Fe supermarket. Those bright lights make me feel like a junkie interrogated by the cops, like I have to act as happy as a cudchewing cow or they'll think I'm up to trouble. I've vowed to never stand in line like an asshole ever again.

But tomorrow, tomorrow I will work again. To grind the reality of my impotency into my religion. It's been two years now. The potential for pleasure, for creating life, still lives on in my head if not in my body. There's no denying what my years have taught: all of life is contained in dreams of youth. But there's no place to hide in the desert, even hellish knowledge finds you, finds your secret stash of good faith. This devastating summer won't allow fruition. Vitality is baked to irretreivability. I must buttress myself against optimism. Realization must be achieved, if necessary, by soul-death.

The next evening, I call the call-girl agency and Danielle answers.

"How dare you treat me like a whore!"

Resignation comes naturally. A lie easily told. I'm so flattered to have made an impression. "Maybe I should go with another, dear?"

"Fuck you."

"Danielle? Danielle?"

The phone is readjusted. I know she is there.

"Please come tonight. Don't go to Rocketboom."

"You're jealous for me."

"I have something to show you. A romantic thing."

"How sweet. I didn't think any man looked at me but to smack me around."

"Come late. In natural clothes. A romance for you."

"You don't like the nurse?"

"No. Come as you are."

I hear the snapping of gum. "Whatever you want. It's your money."

I've decided to take her to the desert orchard, that absurd Eden. We walk when it is still dark, not yet four a.m. It is a three-mile hike and I've brought along a Jack Daniel's bottle filled with wellwater. With her company the hike is short and I hope she feels the same. We arrive at Madre Hill. The east side holds the expected: desert murder. But on the other side, because of some bizarre orientation of the weather, dew collects, enough to keep grass and trees in business. We circle around the Hill and see grass sprouting between grains of sand. Gnarled trees lean diagonally from the hillside, stark stumps against the wan purple sky offering disfigured dwarf-fruits. Danielle is charmed. I wink when I see her sniffing a fruit for its strange odor.

"Rare beauty stills us."

She takes off her shoes and walks among the spare grass. "Every grain of sand is a world." She holds her hands aloft as if practicing a dance. I'm sure I glow with appreciation. When is the last time this desert ever saw a maiden, a real maiden, dance.

"If you ever quote Blake again I'll fall in love with you."

"I didn't even know that was Blake. I thought it was my fourth grade teacher."

"But Blake was wrong. Most of the sand is grain, plain and useless. Not at all a world. But the corner of the sand, the infinitesimal portion, in that Blake was right. That is *a* world, *our* world."

"Can I take one?" Between the violet shadows and the lemony light of the moon she fondles the skin of a grotesque fruit from the fruitbranch.

"No, no, that fruit is not meant to be eaten."

She plucks one from the tree without pause. A swarm of buzzing bugs start from the skin and scatter aimlessly before converging on a different rotten pulp. "Be fruitflies and multiply," she says. My queen.

She holds the fruit to the moonlight. It is a bruised and stunted apricot. The top is a glorious gold but the bottom is deeply bruised — violet, black and brown.

"It smells awful."

"It ferments in the open sun."

She giggles. "Apricot schnapps." She sniffs deeply and giggles again.

"Yes, my dear." Suddenly, in the distance, a bobcat drunkenly falls from a tree limb. With a thud it hits the ground and we laugh. The cat lumbers to its feet, sniffs at us, and sidesteps into a rock before sauntering off. We sit and pass the fruit back and forth, sniffing its intoxication.

The morning light fans across the sky, an iridescent underside of coral. Nothing compares to the desert sunrise; how it spills over the hills and through the valleys like pent-up floods released. I grab Danielle's hand and we begin to run. She crams the fruit into her pocket and jogs easily, in better shape than me.

"Why are we running?"

"It'll be stifling in less than twenty minutes." The growing heat smothers the nightbirds. The quiet grows ominous. As it peeks from the hill-lip, the first burnishing sunglow takes eight and half minutes to reach the Earth. You can time it exactly because that's the moment you feel blasted by radioactive detonation.

Mojave

At home, safe beneath the shuddering air conditioner, she cuts the apricot into pieces, sniffs a slice and then eats it.

"Do you want some?" she asks.

"No, thank you. I'm happy with my beer."

She munches meditatively. "It's good. Have some."

She passes me a small piece which I eat.

"Do I look drunk?" she asks. "That bobcat was funny."

"Danielle, I want you to consider moving in with me. Sharing my palace until you leave Iceberg."

"OK."

"OK? That's it?"

She shrugs, "I like you, I guess. It doesn't bother me that you can't get it up. It makes me feel safe. I never really had a man that did it for me anyway."

I feel a rush of supreme love. "Well, I'm glad. Though in time I'd suggest you pack up and leave. This is no kind of place for a decent life."

She joins me on the couch and puts an arm around my shoulder. "Where am I going? I got nowhere to be and no place'll have me."

"Is it because of the sirens? The boy sirens."

She pops a last piece of fruit into her mouth and screws up her face. "Sirens?"

"The hidden arias, the music of the sand."

No recognition crosses her face.

"There's no singing boys like there are girls?"

"Nope. I don't even know what you're talking about, Sam."

"Well, what the hell are you looking for here?"

She shrugs and gives a wry smile as if to say, of the two of us, I'm the crazy one.

"I don't know. Some big money."

She cracks up at her own joke. But I'm not buying it.

"Come on, now."

"I don't know. Does it matter? I couldn't tell you even if I knew." She walks into the bathroom, *her* new bathroom.

No dream! I felt bad for her like I feel bad for barren women. I am afraid again. The prostitution. The beatings. It can mean only one thing.

I follow her and find her drawing a bath, filling the tub slowly with claypot wellwater. She uses enough drinking water for two weeks.

"But what will be your new dream? Young ladies must have dreams. Webs of adopted children? Pets that talk the cool of Canadian winter?"

She sheds her clothes and lounges on the edge of the porcelain. Her long legs slip beneath the water. Water giggles above wiggling toes. "Stop being silly. We'll leave here."

I am on my knees, too afraid to touch. "Is that the dream? Or we leave to find a new dream?"

She slides into the water as if donning a luxurious fur coat. Watching the concentration on her face as she dips below the surface is like watching a baby's baptism.

She surfaces and sputters gracefully. Two hands slide across her slick slimy face and through her clumped hair. "You're so stupid. There is no dream. We *came* here to leave together, so we'll leave. You don't have to plan dreaming. Dreaming just happens."

Shocked to the quick, I am not able to understand this wisdom, pristine simplicity. Whatever it means is beyond verbal assault. She opens her arms and I abandon myself fully-clothed into water. I cry in gratitude on her soap-shiny shoulder: "I thought we came here to die…"

"On no…" She laughs the laugh of naughty real-life females, a mythological liquidy sparkle, "…that dream got used-up. That was the fake dream."

Self-portrait

Catfish Karkowsky lives in Memphis, where he attended The University of Memphis.